"We don't have a relationship."

His eyes sharpened. "You sure about that?" Seth's expression was tight. "I need to stay away from you. Until this thing with McGregor is done with. For everyone's sake."

She swallowed the knot in her throat. She was shaking from her head to her toes. "Then stay away."

A muscle in his jaw flexed. "Believe me," he said. "I have tried." He slowly moved around the island until he stopped in front of her, trapping her in the corner where she stood near the sink.

She couldn't seem to look away from his blue, blue eyes.

"And I can't," he finished in a low voice.

Her lips parted.

His head dipped toward hers, his lips grazing hers, lighter than his whisper. "Don't trust me, Hayley. Be stronger than I am."

A sound she didn't recognize slid from her throat. Her hands curled into fists against the counter on one side of her and the cool edge of the old-fashioned apron sink on the other. "I'm not strong."

One Night in Weaver...

ALLISON LEIGH

First published in Great Britain 2015
by Mills & Boon, an imprint of Harlequin (UK) Limited,
Large Print edition 2015
Eton House, 18-24 Paradise Road,
Richmond, Surrey, TW9 1SR

ISBN: 978-0-263-26002-1

Harlequin (UK) Limited's policy is to use papers that are natural, renewable and recyclable products and made from wood grown in sustainable forests. The logging and manufacturing processes conform to the legal environmental regulations of the country of origin.

Printed and bound in Great Britain
by CPI Antony Rowe, Chippenham, Wiltshire

ALLISON LEIGH

A frequent name on bestseller lists, Allison Leigh's high point as a writer is hearing from readers that they laughed, cried or lost sleep while reading her books. She's blessed with an immensely patient family who doesn't mind (much) her time spent at her computer and who gives her the kind of love she wants her readers to share in every page. Stay in touch at allisonleigh.com and on Twitter, @allisonleighbks.

For my family.

Prologue

He really *was* exceptionally good looking.

A good six feet tall. Probably more. Dark brown hair that she suspected he kept cut short because it might have the tendency to curl into girlish prettiness if he didn't. Bright blue eyes that seemed startling in contrast to the dark hair.

The first time she'd seen him was at least a year ago, in the Weaver Community Park. Running and looking far more natural at it than she did. After that, the chance of catching a glimpse of him provided a major incentive for Hayley to drag herself to the park a few times every week, where she would meet up with Sam Dawson, her running partner and one of her best friends.

Sam ran every day. And trained with weights. She was a fitness fiend; she claimed it was because she needed to keep up with the guys in the sheriff's department, where she was the only female on the force. Hayley figured that even if Sam worked behind a teller's window in a bank all day long, she'd still be in the park every morning, snow or shine, doing her thing. Hayley was thirty-five. Too old to kid herself that she ran for the pleasure of it. No. Hayley joined Sam a few times a week because she liked being able to fit into her suits and still indulge in her favorite cinnamon rolls from Ruby's diner.

And she liked catching glimpses of *him*.

The man—she knew his name was Seth Banyon because she'd heard it around town—obviously subscribed to Sam's methodology, though.

The man was a walking advertisement for the benefits of physical fitness.

She'd also seen him around town. Often at Shop-World, where his grocery cart tended to be more heavily loaded than hers. He always seemed to buy the same things. A six-pack of beer. Giant loaves of bread. Steak. Bacon. Eggs. Several packaged frozen meals.

Her cart, on the other hand, contained fresh vegetables and fruit. And never a steak, despite Weaver, Wyoming, pretty much being located in the center of the beef universe. The only item their carts ever had in common was coffee. Same brand. Hers, whole bean. His, already ground.

"Bring you another cosmo, Dr. Templeton?"

Hayley gathered her wandering thoughts and blinked once, focusing on the cocktail waitress who'd stopped next to the small high-top that Hayley was hogging all to herself.

She didn't ordinarily drink cocktails; usually she stuck with a glass of white wine, which suited the expectations the citizens of Weaver had for their local psychologist, Hayley Templeton, PhD. And she certainly never drank alone.

Nor did she ogle men bellied up to the bar of Colbys, no matter how nicely they filled the rears of their faded blue jeans and the shoulders of their long-sleeved T-shirts, or how long it had been since she'd had a man's arms around her.

One who wasn't related by blood, at any rate.

She pushed aside the thought of her family. They were the reason she was there in Colbys, alone, trying her hand at the age-old practice of drowning her sorrows in alcohol.

"Yes, please." She offered up the two glasses that she'd already emptied, surreptitiously steadying her hands by propping her elbows on the tabletop. If she'd had anywhere else to go to wallow in her liquor-glazed misery, she would have.

But tonight, Colbys was going to have to suffice.

All around her, people were knotted together in clusters, still celebrating the passing of the old year and the arrival of the new, even though New Year's Eve was two evenings past.

She'd expected to still be celebrating, too. At home in Braden, some thirty miles away, with her family.

Celebrating not just the fresh new year. But a fresh, new beginning for the Templeton family.

The *entire* Templeton family.

She was a good therapist. But obviously not good enough to heal the rift in her own family. A rift that—according to her father—she was actually *causing* by continuing to harbor the enemy. His words.

She sighed and let her gaze drift back to Seth Banyon. One foot was propped casually on the metal rod that ran the length of the bar near the floor. He was leaning on his forearms, which rested atop the glossy wooden surface.

Unlike ninety percent of the men—and

women—in here, who wore cowboy boots on their feet and cowboy hats on their heads, his head was bare and he wore sturdy black work boots. They weren't exactly shined.

But they weren't covered in the ranch dust that was typical of the boots around Weaver, either. He was a security guard out at Cee-Vid, the consumer electronics and video gaming company located on the edge of town. She knew that about him only because her other best friend, Jane Cohen, had once mentioned it.

The waitress set Hayley's fresh cocktail on the table, nearly making her jump. Fortunately, the girl—Hayley knew her name, but she was having the hardest time remembering it—didn't seem to notice. Instead, she just hovered there for a moment, asking if Hayley was *sure* she didn't want to order some food.

Hayley knew Colbys' menu like the back of her hand because Jane owned the place. And just to keep Olive—*that* was her name!—from asking this same question for a sixth time, Hayley ordered a grilled chicken sandwich even though the thought of food on top of all the alcohol was vaguely nauseating.

But Olive beamed, obviously satisfied that she'd done her part to keep the good town therapist supplied in food as well as drink, and headed back behind the busy bar, where she punched in Hayley's order.

Hayley's gaze drifted back to Seth. He'd turned around so that he was no longer leaning over the bar but leaning back against it and facing her.

And his blue, blue gaze collided with hers.

Flushing a little, she quickly looked down at her drink. She took too hasty a sip and couldn't stifle the choking cough that resulted.

She recovered quickly enough but felt her cheeks grow even warmer at the sight of the faint smile hovering around Seth's lips. Obviously, he'd seen.

She was glad when Olive returned with her

sandwich and a glass of water, and Hayley had a valid reason to stare down at her table; she felt as if she was still an awkward sixteen-year-old in the Braden High School cafeteria, where she'd always been too shy to do anything else. Such as participate in an actual conversation with those around her.

She cut the thick sandwich in half and took a bite, chewing determinedly even though her stomach rolled dangerously as she swallowed.

She definitely should have stuck to wine.

She set the sandwich back on the thick white plate and reached for her water glass, only to knock her knuckles into it and send it teetering. Stifling an oath, she tried to right the cup but only succeeded in finishing the job of tipping it on its side, sending ten ounces of water and ice right into her lap.

"Sugarnuts," she hissed under her breath as she grabbed napkins from the dispenser on the table and swabbed futilely at the cascade.

"Here." A white bar towel appeared in her peripheral vision. She glanced at the long-fingered, square hand holding it and, realizing who'd come to her rescue, reluctantly looked up.

Wanting to sink through the floor, she avoided Seth's gaze, snatched the towel from him and sopped up the water in her lap. It was dripping off the padded chair onto the scuffed, wooden floor and he smoothly dropped a handful of paper napkins on the puddle before it spread any farther.

"Thanks," she muttered.

Without invitation, he pulled out the other chair tucked against the small table and sat, placing his beer bottle next to her cosmo. "You going to eat all those?"

He had a drawl that wasn't from Wyoming. And while she was busy noticing that, he'd already dived in to her French fries.

"Help yourself," she said in a dry tone.

His lips tilted and his gaze drifted over her

face as he reached for another sliver of crispy, fried potato. "Thanks. You're not usually here by yourself."

"Ummm...no." The bite of chicken sandwich sat heavily somewhere in the middle of her chest. Because the contents of her water glass were soaking through her jeans and the pile of napkins on the floor, she reached for the cosmopolitan again, even though her head was already swimming.

She didn't dare make too much of his observation about her being here tonight. Sooner or later, everyone came through Colbys. It was a mainstay in Weaver. Just because he happened to notice something about her didn't mean diddly.

He studied her for a moment. Then he swallowed another one of her French fries, wiped his salty fingers on his jeans and reached across the table, his hand extended. "Seth Banyon."

She automatically shook his hand. "I know."

The admission escaped and her face turned hotter than ever. She pulled her hand quickly away from his and managed not to rub her palm on her own jeans even though the temptation was strong. “Hayley Templeton,” she said abruptly.

Why was it that she only felt truly confident with strangers when they were her patients? If *she* were her patient, she’d assign herself some homework about that. Small steps designed to increase her comfort in an area always outside her comfort zone.

“I know. *Dr.* Hayley Templeton.” He wrapped his long fingers around his beer bottle and tilted it to his lips. “The shrink,” he added when he set the bottle down again.

“The psychologist,” she corrected.

If anything, he looked even more amused, a faint dimple appearing in his lean cheek, though he managed not to smile outright. “Heard Jane was off visitin’ someone for the holidays, but where’s your other friend? The blonde without a lick o' Christmas spirit who gave me a ticket the other day?"

Despite her woozy head, she instantly knew who he was talking about. "Sam has plenty of Christmas spirit," she countered defensively.

"Well, *Sam* still wrote me a speeding ticket on Christmas Eve. Probably gonna cost me a couple hundred bucks."

"Probably because you shouldn't have been speeding."

His lips twitched slightly. If he was concerned over the ticket or the ensuing cost, he didn't particularly look it.

He knew Hayley's name but not Sam's? Being the only female deputy sheriff around, she stood out even more than Hayley, the psychologist.

She pushed aside the thought and picked up her sandwich, only to set it back down again. She plucked a French fry from the pile and nibbled on the end instead. They were crispy. Salty. Still hot and exactly the way she liked them.

But her stomach still didn't seem thrilled at the prospect of food. She forced down the rest of the fry anyway and wiped her fingers on a fresh napkin. It was the last one in the dispenser. The rest were on the floor performing sop-up duty.

When a burst of laughter came from one of the nearby tables, she made herself meet Seth's eyes because she *was* a grown woman and no longer a socially awkward teen. "What are *you* doing in here alone?" Unfortunately, the question came out more blunt than flirtatious, and she wished the floor would just swallow her whole.

He didn't answer. Merely lifted his beer bottle and finished off the contents. Then he set the bottle back down alongside her cosmo, and his knuckles grazed hers. She went hot in spots that didn't show from the outside and was glad for that. He reached for his wallet, pulled out a few dollars and left them on the table and filched several more French fries, which he ate in one gulp as he stood.

Maybe if she'd spent more time developing a social life instead of her career, she wouldn't get all hot and bothered by the briefest, most unintentional contact imaginable.

"You have someone to drive you home?" he asked in his deep voice. Drive sounded more like *drahve.* He was looking at her cocktail glass.

She managed, somehow, to loosen her tight fingers from around the stem and blood reentered her fingertips. "I'm walking." She lifted the sandwich again, but her roiling stomach kept her from taking the charade of hunger any further.

"It's snowin' outside."

"It often does around here this time of year," she said with such blitheness she was actually impressed with herself.

"I'll drive you." He lifted the sandwich out of her suddenly lax fingers and set it on the plate. Before she could gather her wits, he'd grabbed the towel from her lap and cupped his hand around her elbow. “Come on.”

She stood, because, well, what else could she do considering the way he was tugging her off the barstool? “I don’t want to go home,” she blurted, the fake blitheness beyond her reach again. Her grandmother, Vivian, was staying with her. And facing her would mean admitting what a disaster Hayley’s latest attempt to visit her parents had been. Avoiding that embarrassment was the very reason why Hayley had been warming the barstool in Colbys in the first place.

Seth dropped the towel on the table. “Then we’ll go to my place.”

She stared at him. She couldn’t help it. “And do what?”

His gaze drifted over her face. “I think we can find something to entertain us. Don’t you?”

Her belly lurched. There was no mistaking his meaning.

His lips twitched slightly as he looked pointedly at the table. “You going to pay your check? Or does your friend let you eat and drink for free?”

Truth be told, Jane never wanted Hayley to pay for anything in Colbys, but Hayley always insisted. Flushing darker than ever, she snatched her purse from the back of the barstool and left a wad of cash on the table to cover her tab plus a tip.

“All right, then.” His faint smile widened a bit as he held out her coat for her.

Swallowing hard, Hayley slid her arms into the sleeves. Seth’s hands lingered on her shoulders for a moment. Something was going wrong with her breathing. “My jeans are wet,” she said stupidly.

His smile widened. His teeth were white and very straight, except for the faintest gap between his two front teeth.

"I think we can do something about that, too," he said leaning forward near her ear.

Then he spread his palm across the small of her back and nudged her gently toward the door.

Head spinning, not knowing what else to do and not wanting to do anything else anyway, Hayley mindlessly put one foot in front of the other and walked out of the bar with him.

Chapter One

Three months later

His jaw going so tight that it actually ached, Seth stared at the other man. "You have *got* to be kidding me."

Tristan Clay's calm expression didn't change; his light blue eyes looked glacial. "Do I look like I'm joking?"

Seth clenched his teeth to keep from spitting out an oath. There was a time and a place for that, and here in his boss's home while Tristan and his wife hosted a joint wedding shower for their nephew and his fiancée was definitely not it.

Fortunately, the honorees, Casey Clay and Jane Cohen, were on the far side of the room and were the focus of everyone else's attention. But Seth still kept his voice down. "I don't believe you've fallen for this—" he hesitated, revising the words he wanted to say "—*story* that Jason McGregor has amnesia."

"That'll be up to Dr. Templeton to determine," Tristan said smoothly. "She'll be the one treating him. But the condition does occur. My own brother dealt with it once upon a time." He smiled suddenly and lifted his beer mug in salute when he overheard Casey say something about him hosting the party. "Thank my wife, Hope," Tristan announced loudly to the assembled guests. "Everyone knows she's the brains behind this gig."

Laughter and smiles followed as Hope Clay,

easily as beautiful as women half her age, rolled her eyes and continued nudging wrapped gifts toward Casey and Jane.

Seth's contribution to the effort had been a case of microbrew from some dinky little startup out in Arizona that Casey had a liking for. The fact that his coworker was marrying the owner of a bar and could get all the beer he wanted had already been laughed about.

"Whatever happened with your brother is one thing. But McGregor should be facing murder charges," Seth told Tristan, not for the first time. "Not your hired shrink's couch."

His boss didn't blink. On the surface, Tristan Clay was the brilliant mind that had started Cee-Vid as a little video gaming company several decades ago and built it into a hugely successful player in the world of consumer electronics and gaming. But more important, behind the company's front, he was the number-two guy at Hollins-Winword, a secret organization with an even longer history of black ops and international security.

Cee-Vid, where Seth and Casey ostensibly worked, was pretty much a household name.

Hollins-Winword, though, was a closely guarded secret that not even the real employees of Cee-Vid knew about.

"Dr. Templeton isn't my shrink," Tristan said in a low voice. "She's an impartial professional whose expertise and discretion were good enough to get this whole operation approved in the first place. She knows only what she needs to know about HW in order to do her job well."

Seth's fists curled, frustration ticking like a bomb inside his gut. "And how's that supposed to help Jon and Manny?" They'd been McGregor's partners up until the point when their bodies had been discovered in a Honduran hut six months ago. McGregor had been nowhere to be found until a few months later, and only then because he'd been picked up in Mississippi on some traffic stop. The Hollins-Winword agent had been using one of his known aliases.

It was the one kernel that kept sticking in Seth's teeth. If McGregor hadn't been using the alias, he would likely still be in the wind. And the field agent had never been a stupid man, even if Seth did consider him guilty of murdering his partners. "You think that's going to help their grieving families? Knowing the person responsible is getting *counseling*?"

Tristan's lips thinned. He took his responsibilities—both public and private—very seriously. "Their families will never know the entire truth about their deaths, whether or not Jason was responsible," he said flatly. "And you know it. That's a price everyone who signs on with us pays. Whether someone dies as a hero or not, the complete truth stays unsung. If it didn't, we would've been out of business before you were a spark in your daddy's eyes."

Seth's jaw went even tighter because he did

know that. "When I signed on with the agency, there weren't any people in my life to worry about me. Any people to lie to." So that decision had been easy.

Jon, Manny and Jason, though, all had family. Parents. Siblings. And all of them believed the cover story. That their sons and brothers had been ex-pats cranking out a meager living as farmers in a tiny corner of Central America. They didn't know they'd really been there to feed intel to the authorities about a local drug king who'd branched out into human trafficking. Not even Hollins-Winword's considerable resources had been able to prove that their covers had been blown, a circumstance that would have laid their murders squarely on the drug king's doorstep.

Instead, the entire situation was still surrounded with question marks even all these months later. The recent discovery that the drug king had also been funding suspected terrorists had only upped the stakes where McGregor was concerned.

"If your father hadn't been killed when you were a pup, you wouldn't have signed on with us?" Tristan's gaze was steady. "You honestly believe that?"

Seth grimaced. His father's unavenged death when he was eighteen still haunted him, though after twenty years, he mostly managed not to think about it.

Thankfully, Tristan left the subject of Seth's dad alone. "We have bullets recovered from their bodies that we haven't been able to trace back to a specific weapon, much less Jason's. That's it. That leaves us with his memories. Locked up in his head or willfully hidden away. When that question is resolved, then we'll take our next step. In the meantime, we got him back from the Feds only by calling in a boatload of favors. I don't want anything screwing it up or he'll get yanked back under government detention for God knows how long while they figure out what to do with him, and we'll lose any chance we've ever had of learning the truth of what really happened in Central America."

"Maybe that's where he belongs," Seth said under his breath. "Whatever he ended up doing down there, he started out with two partners who were killed. And *you're* harboring him in a comfy little safe house right here in Weaver."

"You were friends with Jon and Manny—"

"*Were* being the operative word."

Tristan set his mug on the chest-high fireplace mantel behind them, clamped his hand over Seth's shoulder and guided him out of the room and to the front door. "Go home," he advised quietly. "Get your head back on straight. The likelihood of there ever being a public court case about this situation is slim to none." The federal government would never allow some things—such as their off-the-books arrangement with Hollins-Winword to handle some of their dirty work—to see the light of day.

"So he just walks," Seth said between his teeth.

Tristan's grip hardened. He was a good twenty-five years older than Seth, but there was little doubt the man could have taken Seth—former US Army Ranger or not—right to the ground if he so chose. At least, he could have done a good job trying. "If he's innocent, yes." Tristan lowered his hand. "You've got the choice, Seth. You want to leave the organization, say the word."

"I could take everything I know to the media."

Tristan snorted, his eyes filling with honest-to-God mirth. "Honor runs thicker in your veins than blood does, kid. Why else do you think I recruited you out of the Rangers?"

"There's no honor in letting a man get away with murder."

"He hasn't gotten away with it yet, has he?" Tristan's voice was smooth. "Until I got him transferred here to my watch, he was wearing leg irons in a military prison. But that cozy safe house you're all pissed off about now still doesn't unlock from the inside." He pulled open the door.

The soft, feminine gasp that greeted them didn't stump the older man for even a second as his face creased into a wide, welcoming smile. "Dr. Templeton. My wife was just wondering when you'd be arriving." He stepped back, his arm wide in invitation. "Come in. Can't have the maid of honor standing out on the front porch."

Hayley Templeton stared back at them above the large gift-wrapped box she was holding, her dark brown eyes looking like melted chocolate in the dwindling sunset. But her gaze instantly flicked away from Seth's like a skittish firefly.

It had been that way ever since that night at Colbys several months ago.

Her soft lips stretched into a smile that wasn't entirely steady. "Mr. Clay," she greeted. "I'm so sorry I'm late." Her gaze flicked to Seth's again. "I, was, um, was tied up with a new patient."

"It's Tristan, Hayley. I've told you that before. And patients come first. We all certainly understand that." He looked over his shoulder for a moment when his wife called his name. He lifted his hand in acknowledgment before turning back to Hayley. His gaze took in Seth, as well. "Seth, before you head out, help the doctor here with that gift of hers and make sure she has a drink, would you?" Then he excused himself, his easy smile still in place.

Hayley's, though, turned even more ragged at the edges and her eyes still wouldn't meet Seth's for more than a nanosecond. "I'm a big girl," she said quickly. "I don't need help with the gift."

"Much less getting a drink."

Her cheeks turned pink. "A gentleman wouldn't remind me of that."

"I never said I was a gentleman." But his father hadn't raised him to be a complete cretin, either, despite their male-only household. “Don’t worry so much, Doc. You had a few too many that night,” he said with a shrug. “Plenty of us have done the same at one time or another.” Without waiting for permission, he lifted the box out of her hands and turned to carry it inside.

“Well, *I* don’t make a habit of it,” she muttered as she closed the door and hurried to keep up with him. “Not drinking too much and certainly not going home with strange men.”

“Never said you did.” He glanced at her. “If you had bothered to return either of the messages I left you after that night, I might have had a chance to reassure you of that.” He entered the crowded living room, set the box on the floor next to the other gifts that overflowed from the low table in front of the couch where Jane and Casey were seated and edged back out of the room.

Hayley was waiting where he’d left her on the perimeter of the room. Nobody else seemed to have noticed her arrival, but he was still more than a little surprised when she turned and trotted after him as he headed back to the foyer and the front door. "Seth, wait."

He stopped, turned and raised his brows.

She looked pained. "I should have." Her lips pressed together for a moment. "Returned your message." She quickly looked over her shoulder. "Could we take this outside, at least?"

"Don't want the masses to know you socialize with a lowly security guard?"

She gave him a look. "Don't be ridiculous."

"Then what's your problem, Doc? You hightailed it out of my place before the sun came up the next morning."

"I was embarrassed!" Her voice had risen a bit and she looked annoyed again. She ran her hand over her head, smoothing back her ponytail even though it already looked perfectly smooth to him.

Irritatingly, his memory filled in just how silky it was.

Then she caught his sleeve and pulled him out the front door and onto the porch. She closed the door behind them and immediately let go to move several feet away, where she crossed her arms.

No point in remembering how silky her hair was when she wanted nothing to do with him.

Even though they were outside, she still lowered her voice. "I was embarrassed," she said again. "I've never found myself in...in that position before, and I handled it poorly. And I, well, I apologize for that. I meant no offense."

He hadn't been offended.

Disappointed a little. Maybe more than a little.

But he was thirty-eight years old and he told himself he was too jaded to get upset over a woman. Particularly one as beautiful and out-of-reach as Dr. Hayley Templeton. He shrugged again. "No sweat. The only reason I left those messages in the first place was to make sure you were okay." That was true enough.

She blinked. Whatever she'd expected him to say, it was obviously not that. "Um…okay, then. So, we can just forget it ever happened?"

"Yup." He started down the wide, shallow porch steps but looked back at her. She was wearing a pale gray pencil skirt that ended just below her knees and a white long-sleeved blouse that was buttoned to just below the hollow of her slender throat.

Aside from her tall, shocking-pink high heels, she looked prim and proper as if she'd just come from a session with a patient, even though it was eight o'clock on a Saturday evening. All he could think about was how fun it would be to get her all mussed up. To finish what they'd never gotten to start the night she'd gone home with him.

But she'd already made it clear that she wanted nothing to do with him. She was not interested.

And now, according to Tristan, her latest patient was one Jason McGregor.

He ruthlessly uprooted the idea germinating in the back of his mind. She had a spotless reputation around town. And she had to be exceptionally good at what she did to earn Tristan Clay's confidence. She would never betray a patient's confidentiality to Seth, even if he could get into her confidence. Which, considering everything, was unlikely.

Not to mention the fact that Tristan would have his head if he tried. Few people earned Seth's respect, particularly ones with that much money. But his boss was one of them. He disagreed like hell with the man over McGregor, but that didn't change that one basic fact.

"Better get inside," he advised. "Maid of honor and all."

She put one hand on the door latch. "Are you working at Cee-Vid tonight or something?"

Or something. "No." He wondered why she

bothered with small talk. Why she didn't go inside.

And he wondered *why* he wondered. "Not in the mood for a party." A breeze drifted over them, playing with her silky ponytail and making her blouse flutter against her body. He wasn't a cretin, but he was a man. And regardless of what had happened three months ago—or had not happened, to be more precise—he'd have to be dead not to appreciate the here-and-gone-again whisper of lace and the gentle curve beneath that thin white fabric.

"Stay away from the cosmopolitans, Dr. Templeton," he advised, backing down the last of the porch steps. His lips twisted in a smile. "The next guy you're with might not be as much of a *gentleman* as I was."

Intent on escaping this unsettling man, Hayley was halfway inside the Clays' house again when Seth's words penetrated enough to make sense—and annoyance swept through her.

Maybe she hadn't handled that night with him very well, but he hadn't exactly turned out to be Mr. Charming, either.

She looked back.

He was already striding across the long driveway crowded with vehicles of every make and model, his dark head lowered slightly like that of a man deep in thought.

Behind her, she could hear the sounds of the wedding shower that she'd have been on time for if not for taking on a new patient at Tristan's own request.

Moving abruptly, she went back outside, quickly closing the door again. Jane Cohen was her best friend. If anyone would understand, it was Jane.

Then Hayley hurried down the steps, her high-heeled pumps clicking on the paved driveway as she half-jogged after Seth. Because of her tardiness to the party, she was parked at the tail end of the long line of cars. But Seth, who'd parked much closer to the house, had already reached his dusty gray pickup truck, so she quickened her pace.

Running with Sam in the park a few times a week properly equipped with appropriate shoes was a snap compared to jogging down a crowded driveway in four-inch heels and a narrow skirt. "Seth!"

He showed no sign of hearing her as he started up his truck and inched his way out from between the other cars. She cursed when her heel caught on an uneven spot and her ankle twisted painfully.

Feeling wholly undignified—the same way she'd felt waking alone in Seth's bed months ago with a splitting headache and wearing nothing but her bra and panties—she stopped and leaned against the hood of the SUV next to her. She reached down to tug off her shoe and gingerly rotated her foot, watching Seth's taillights as he drove away.

"Brilliant, Dr. Templeton. Just...brilliant."

Sighing, she fit her shoe back in place and, limping only a little, made her way back to the house and the celebration.

Jane and Casey were finished opening the gifts by the time Hayley slipped into the living room. Tristan's wife had vacated her spot on the floor next to the couch in order to clear away the piles of discarded wrappings, so Hayley made her way to it, sitting down on her knees because that was the only position her skirt allowed. Now that the gifts were dealt with, most of the guests were milling around talking and filling their plates with food from the buffet set up across the room.

"Sorry I'm so late."

Casey was busy talking with one of his numerous cousins and Jane waved away the apology, her diamond engagement ring sparkling. "No worries," she said, smiling. "This is the tenth party we've had."

"Second," Hayley corrected her. "And you've got one more party next weekend to live through, remember? Your bachelorette party."

Jane's grin was impish as she leaned toward Hayley. "Remind me why I didn't think running off to Vegas was a good idea."

Hayley chuckled softly. "Because even in your supposedly modern, independent heart, you want to walk up that church aisle and pledge your troth in front of everyone."

"*Everyone* is right." Casey turned and joined the conversation. "We have more people coming than can fit into the church."

Casey's father, Daniel, obviously had overheard. "A common enough problem where Clay family weddings are concerned," he commented before taking an enormous bite of the chocolate cake on his plate.

"Well, you're related to half the town," Jane told Casey. "So I guess it's not really a surprise."

"Not *half* the town." Casey gestured toward Hayley. "Last I checked, we weren't on the same family tree. So I know there's at least one."

Hayley laughed along with the others. But inside, she felt a pang. The Templeton family wasn't quite as extensive as the Clays, but there were still a good many of them. She was just persona non grata with her father right now. And after several months of trying, she was beginning to fear she'd never get him to see reason.

She pushed away the depressing thought and gestured at the array of gifts spread across the coffee table and beyond. Some were very traditional, like the set of towels she'd chosen. And some were less so, like the case of beer she could see sitting on the other side of Casey. "You're going to be writing thank-you notes until next Christmas."

"Don't remind me." Jane's voice was rueful. "I didn't work the bar last night and—"

"She spent the entire time writing out thank-you notes from the shower her sister gave her last week in Colorado," Casey interrupted, "instead of lavishing attention on her fiancé."

Jane rolled her eyes. "You poor soul, you."

Casey smiled and kissed Jane's nose. "You made up for it this morning."

Jane pushed him away, laughing and blushing at the same time. "What am I going to do with you?"

"Marry him in two weeks, I'd say," Hayley offered.

"Speaking of... Are you *sure* you don't mind staying at our place to watch Moose while we're on our honeymoon? Every time we've tried to leave him with one of Casey's relatives, Moose is either terrified of the other animals there, or his hosts end up terrified of him eating them out of furniture, doors and shoes."

"I'm positive."

"Your grandmother won't mind?"

"Vivian has already said she'll be glad to have my place to herself for a few weeks." After having her grandmother staying with her for the past six months, maybe they would both benefit from some distance. When Hayley had rented the place, she hadn't done so with a long-term guest in mind.

"She's still going to come to the wedding?"

Hayley shrugged. "That's what she says. But I've learned not to count on anything until it actually occurs." Ever since Vivian had come to stay with her, she'd changed her mind about doing something she'd said she would at least a half-dozen times. "Vivian's a law unto herself." In that, Hayley's father's assessment of his mother was spot-on. "Considering the brick wall my dad and Uncle David have put up to the idea of seeing her, I'm really not sure why she hasn't gone home to Pittsburgh by now."

"She likes your company?" Jane's voice was amused.

"Or else she just likes having someone around to bug about their love life. Yesterday she actually told me I'd be better off finding a real date for your wedding since I wasn't getting any younger."

"What'd you tell her?"

Hayley made a face. "That I didn't think I was in danger of drying up into an old prune just because there's no man of interest around."

But even as she said the words, she knew they weren't true.

There was a man of interest.

Seth Banyon.

A man with whom she'd had a one-night stand three months ago.

A one-night stand she couldn't even remember.

Chapter Two

"You threw a great bachelorette party, Hayley." J. D. Forrest gave Hayley a hug before throwing her slender arm around Jane, who was standing beside her. "Are you *sure* you want to marry my little brother? He's kind of a pain in the patoot."

Jane's eyes glinted with humor. "Pretty sure. He has a few good points."

J.D. grinned. "Yeah, but I'm his sister, and I definitely do *not* want to know what they are." She finished wrapping a lightweight scarf around her neck and leaned forward to kiss

Jane's cheek. "Seriously, you've made him one happy camper, which makes those of us who love the guy happy, too." Moving with her typical quickness, she started for the door of Colbys, where the party had been held. "And we're all hoping you can do something about his wardrobe. He wears the ugliest shirts any of us have ever seen!" Still smiling, she pushed through the door into the evening.

The moment her future sister-in-law was gone, Jane plopped down onto the nearest chair and covered a yawn with her hand. "Getting married is exhausting."

Hayley started gathering up the glasses scattered around on the tables. "It's not the getting married part that's exhausting. It's the wedding itself and all of the busyness leading up to it." She shook her head when Jane started to push to her feet. "No, no, no, my friend. The only reason I agreed to have your bachelorette party *here* was because you promised to pretend you didn't own the place and agreed to let your employees be guests, not workers. You're not helping me clean up."

Jane collapsed back into her chair. "I could overrule you, you know. I *am* the bride as well as the owner of this establishment."

"You could." Hayley stacked the glasses on a tray and carefully carried them behind the bar, rattling them only a little as she went. "But why? This is one time in your life when you can let your friends do things for *you*. So let us."

"There is no *us*," Jane pointed out. "There's only you, since you refused all the people who offered to hang around and help clean up."

Hayley set down the tray and flipped off the country music that had been playing over the sound system all night. The sudden quiet was welcome. "Sam would have stayed to help if she hadn't gotten called in for duty." Hayley had seen Jane operate the dishwasher behind the bar often enough that she figured she could manage it herself. She began loading glasses onto one of the racks. “Casey’s going to be here to pick you up in a few minutes anyway.”

“But if you need help, you can check—”

“—with Jerry,” Hayley finished, glancing across to the open doorway that led to the restaurant side of the bar and grill, where Jane’s cook was still at it. Even though it was past closing time for the grill, the lights were still on over there and with the music turned off in the bar, she could hear the rattle of dishes and murmur of voices from his late-night customers.

“Okay, so maybe I am a bit of a control freak,” Jane admitted. At the sound of the door opening, she turned and looked over her shoulder.

“Did I actually hear the words ‘control freak’ come out of your lips?” Casey asked as he entered.

Hayley didn’t bother trying to hide her smile as she bent over to slide the rack into the dishwasher.

"You heard nothing of the sort," Jane countered blithely. "The brightness of your neon orange shirt has affected your hearing. Speaking of… Your sister wants me to do something about your shirts."

"Admit it." Casey leaned over his fiancée and kissed her before pulling her to her feet. "The only thing you want to do about my shirts is get me out of them."

"Save it for the honeymoon," Hayley told them. "My innocent ears can't take any more."

"Please." Jane rolled her eyes and ducked under Casey's arm to come around the bar. "Are you *sure* you don't want—?"

"Get out of here." Hayley gave her a hug and a push. "The party is over, so go home. I'll make sure everything's locked up."

"I know. I just—" Jane closed her mouth when Hayley pointedly looked at Casey for help. "Fine. Fine!" Her friend tossed up her hands and went back around the bar. She took the costume tiara that Sam had mockingly insisted she wear during the party and fit it back on her head before joining Casey.

"Think it suits me?"

"Well, you're already the queen of my heart," he drawled, nearly frog-stepping her to the door.

"Oh, brother." Jane sent Hayley a look as they left, but Hayley knew just how deeply in love the two were and once the door finally closed behind them, she couldn't help but sigh a little.

Not with envy. She wasn't envious of her friend's happiness.

But she couldn't help being even more acutely aware of her own solitary life in the face of all of that happiness.

Blowing out a breath, she peeled off her high-heeled boots and wiggled her stocking-clad toes as she went around to each of the tables, picking up paper plates and crumpled napkins and dumping them in a trash bag.

"Looks like you got left holding the bag."

She startled, jerking around at the sound of the deep voice, and somehow managed to spill the trash she'd just collected. She spotted Seth standing in the doorway to the grill. "What are you doing here?"

He held up his plate and fork as if it should have been obvious. "Jerry's got good pecan pie. And I was hungry after working a double."

She hadn't seen him since she'd tried to chase after him at the wedding shower the week before, and she felt as foolish now as she always seemed to feel around him. "Well, the restaurant might have stayed open to serve you, but the bar's closed."

"I gathered that from the girly-looking Closed for Private Function sign taped on the wall." He took a few steps closer anyway. "Didn't know that Colbys was fancy enough for *private functions*."

She crouched to scoop the plates and napkins back into the bag again. "I threw Jane's bachelorette party here." She grimaced when her fingers sank into an unfinished piece of cake but scooped as much as she could into the bag. She wasn't about to tell him that she was the one who'd fashioned the pretty signs. "There's more room for a party here than at my place." Particularly with her grandmother still in residence. And Jane had insisted that if she *had* to have another party in her honor, she wanted it held someplace where she was extremely comfortable.

Hayley rose and wiped her sticky fingers on another paper napkin that she added to the bag. "What did you mean last week—" she pushed the words out before she lost her nerve "—about being a gentleman?"

He forked another bite of pie into his mouth, not seeming surprised by her abruptness. "I said I wasn't."

She finally looked right at him and felt the usual lurch inside her when she did. He was wearing blue jeans and a snug black T-shirt with SECURITY printed in white block letters across the front. "What you said before you left the Clays' party last week. I had the sense you were implying something. I just don't know what."

His vivid blue eyes narrowed slightly. "Afraid you'll have to clue me in, Dr. Templeton."

She frowned at him. "Don't call me that."

"It's what you are." As if he were perfectly at home doing so, he went behind the bar and grabbed a towel and a bottle of spray cleaner. Then he came back around to where she'd dropped the trash and smoothly knelt to wipe up the bits of cake that had landed on the floor.

Feeling stymied, she stared down at the back of his head as he worked. His hair was starting to curl around his nape and the T-shirt tightened across his muscular shoulders every time he moved his arm.

"It's ridiculous to call me that after we've slept together," she said, wishing she didn't feel as uptight about that fact as she did. She was a therapist, for heaven's sake. She was supposed to understand human nature.

"Ah. I get it now."

She wished she did.

He gave the now-clean floor a last buff with the towel and stood. "We didn't. Sleep together. Have sex. Whatever you're thinking that's got your panties in a twist." He left the bottle and towel on the table, tugged the trash bag out of her hand and headed for the uncleared tables. "Not that I didn't have that in mind when we left here that night."

Her face was hot. She knew she ought to tell him to stop cleaning up. She'd hosted the party and cleaning up afterward was her responsibility. "I woke up in your bed!"

"Yep." He glanced at her over his shoulder. "That's where I put you after you passed out. I spent a very uncomfortable night on a couch that's too damn short."

She pulled out a chair and sat. There was no real reason for her knees to feel weak, but they did. "But I thought we—"

"Nope." He gave her a longer look. "Believe me, sweetheart. I'd remember if we had. Call me conceited, but I'd like to think you would, too."

A shiver slid down her spine. "But when I woke up that morning, I wasn't dressed."

He came back to her and placed the half-full bag on the center of the table in front of her. "Unless you managed to strip yourself off while you were dead to the world, you still had on your undies when I put you to bed. I'm sure you weren't naked when you decided to bolt at 4 a.m. either."

Considering how hot her cheeks felt, she probably resembled a summer tomato. And she *had* been wearing her bra and panties when she'd crawled out of his bed. "I didn't bolt."

He deftly twisted the ends of the bag into a knot. "That's what it looked like to me."

"I didn't even know you were there."

His lips twisted. "Yeah, I got that loud and clear when you nearly face-planted on my living room rug in the middle of me kissing you."

"I meant when I *left*."

"Bolted."

She ignored that. "You weren't in bed with me. You weren't anywhere in your apartment at all." She lifted her shoulder as if it was of no consequence. As if his absence that morning hadn't heavily factored into her many reasons for regretting her behavior that night. "I figured you'd left."

"I was sitting on the patio."

She studied him for a moment. "My recall of that night is admittedly limited. But I certainly haven't forgotten that it was the beginning of January. There was at least a foot of snow on the ground. The average high that time of year is below 30 degrees. And you want me to believe you were out on your *patio*. At four in the morning."

"It happens to be the truth. But if you don't want to believe me, you can always talk to my neighbor, Mrs. Carson. Old woman's always looking out her windows watching what's going on." He shrugged. "I was awake. I wanted a cigarette. I was outside. Sitting in a chair, freezing my ass off, smoking said cigarette, when what to my wondering eyes did appear but one doctor skidding her sweet way across the icy parking lot below me like the hounds of hell were on her heels."

He tilted his head slightly. "Convenient to have a friend in the sheriff's department. After I saw you make a call on your cell phone, it took less than three minutes for that cruiser to arrive." His lips kicked up in a smile that didn't reach his eyes. "You stood under the streetlight, stomping your feet to keep warm, but you kept stealing looks back at the apartment building and shaking your head. Face it, Dr. Templeton. You bolted. And ever since then, you've avoided me. I haven't even seen you running in the park lately."

She flinched. His description of that night—that morning—was too detailed. Too accurate. "I told you already. I was embarrassed." She lifted her hand quickly when he began to smile again. "*Not* because you're a security guard at Cee-Vid."

His expression didn't change. "Say whatever it is that helps you sleep at night."

Irritation was building inside her. "I'd make a pretty poor therapist if I judged people by their career choices."

"I didn't take you home that night because I wanted to have my head examined. And that's not why you went with me, either." He planted his hands on the top of the table and leaned closer. His blue eyes were laser-sharp and uncomfortably shrewd. "You were drunk. We both wanted to get laid. Whether it worked out or not is beside the point. I would still be the guy you want to pretend you never went home with."

"I think you're the one with issues about a person's career." Sitting while he stood was unnerving, so she rose, lifting the trash bag by the knot and carrying it over to the door. She would drop it in the bin out back when she locked up and left. "Have you considered talking to someone about that?"

When she turned back to face him, he was sitting on the table, his arms folded across his wide chest. He looked amused. "You offering up your professional services?"

"Not mine," she assured with a lightness she was far from feeling. She crossed back to the table and grabbed the towel and bottle. "It would be unethical."

"Given our…personal connection."

"Yes."

"Pretty unsatisfying, if you ask me." He pushed off the table.

She squeezed the towel in her fist. He suddenly seemed to tower over her. And every time she pulled in a breath, it carried his enticing scent. "Why is that?"

"I don't get to avail myself of the services of the town shrink."

She had to forcibly restrain a shiver when he reached out and slowly tucked some loose strands of hair behind her ear. His hand fell away just as slowly, fingertips grazing her earlobe along the way.

"And I am stuck thinking about the way you felt in my arms, still wishing we'd have had a chance to finish what we started." His gaze dropped to her lips.

She swallowed. Hard. "Seth—" But she stopped, unsure of what she wanted to say. Or do. All she knew was that a huge part of her wanted him to just take the matter into his own hands so that she wouldn't have to.

And how much of a coward did that make her?

His expression suggested that he knew exactly what she was thinking. "See you around, Doc." He turned to go.

Annoyed with herself and her own paralyzing inhibition, she took a step after him. "Wait."

He stopped and looked back.

She reached out, only to forget she was still holding the squirt bottle, and knocked him with it, accidentally spraying the front of his shirt.

Dismayed, all she could do was stare as the droplets immediately began leaching the fabric of its black color. "Oh, sugarnuts! I'm so sorry."

"Sugarnuts?" He let out a bark of laughter. "What the hell kind of curse is that?"

"The kind I didn't get sent to my room for when I was a girl. I'll pay for a new shirt."

He plucked the squirt bottle out of her hand. "I'm glad it wasn't a loaded gun."

She made a face and followed him to the bar as he replaced the bottle where he'd gotten it. "I don't own a gun."

He pointedly looked at his spattered shirt. "Good thing. Being shot in the gut has never been a goal of mine, even when I was in the army."

She blinked a little. Her father had been in the military once upon a time and Seth, with his unshaven jaw and his tumbled hair, didn't exactly smack of the discipline that still ruled her father even all these years later. "I didn't know you were in the army."

"Not something we ever got around to talking about." He rounded the bar again and picked up the plate with his unfinished pie. "Always an adventure with you, Doc. Try not to hurt yourself before you get home."

"What about your shirt?"

"Think I'll live." He was heading for the

breezeway leading back to the restaurant. "I have a closet full of 'em."

"If I can't replace your shirt, maybe I can buy you dinner." The words came out in a rush, surprising them both if the silence that followed was any indication.

He glanced back at her, one eyebrow lifted. "What was that?"

She swallowed, stiffening her spine a little. "You heard me."

His eyes narrowed slightly, which only served to emphasize how dark and thick his eyelashes were. "A bleach-stained T-shirt isn't worth dinner."

"I know," she managed, albeit a shade breathlessly. "But a, um, a gentleman might be worth it."

He let out another short snort of laughter. "Just because I like my women conscious doesn't make me a gentleman." He spread his hand. "But

I'm not gonna turn down a meal that doesn't involve my own microwave."

"Great." She rubbed her damp palms down the sides of her jeans. "Uh...great. Any place you'd like to go?"

A faint smile was playing around his lips. "You don't ask guys out very often, do you." It wasn't a question but an observation.

"Never," she admitted. "Clearly, it's just another thing at which I excel, like ruining a man's work shirt."

His long fingers splayed against the bleach spots across his abdomen. "Why don't we start with lunch? Tomorrow. In the new park out past your office. Willow Park, I think it's called."

She wasn't sure whether to feel elated or deflated. "I haven't been there. I usually go to the community park right here downtown even though it's farther from my office." The park was just across the road from Colbys, in fact. It's where she ran every weekend with Sam. It's where *he* ran, though admittedly, she'd done her level best the past few months to avoid him, just as he'd accused her of doing.

He shrugged. "Just a suggestion. Thought you might relax more if you weren't worried about encountering a lot of people you know."

Now she definitely felt *de*flated. And indignant. "Because you're a security guard?" Her voice was tart. "You'd be less worried about that if you knew how many student loans I am still paying off. And as it happens, I'm not free tomorrow during lunch. But I am for dinner. I'll pick you up. Seven o'clock if that works for you."

His voice, however, was smooth. And amused. "Seven's fine."

Still buoyed by indignation, she nodded sharply. "Good."

But after he disappeared back through the doorway to the restaurant side of Colbys Bar & Grill, she couldn't shake the vague sense that, while she'd finally found the nerve to ask out a man she was admittedly interested in, he'd been the one who'd gotten exactly what he wanted.

She shook her head sharply. Because it was already late and only getting later the longer she dawdled there, she quickly went about upending the chairs on top of the wiped-down tables. Then she swept up the bits of confetti on the floor, unloaded the dishwasher and steeled herself to go through the doorway to the restaurant to let Jerry know she was ready to leave.

Fortunately, only the cook was left. He was sitting at the counter nursing a cup of coffee.

Even better, there was no sign of Seth.

Which left her a solid twenty hours to get used to the idea that everything she'd believed for the past three months where he was concerned had been wrong.

And to get accustomed to the idea that *she* had done something she'd never done before in her life.

Asked a man out on a date.

Chapter Three

"So you *didn't* sleep with pretty boy Seth Banyon." Samantha Dawson sat on the bed in Hayley's room, watching her paw through her closet for something to wear that would be appropriate for her dinner with Seth that evening.

"No. Thank God." She pushed through a few more hangers. "I need to go shopping. The only things I own are suits and blue jeans."

Sam laughed and made a point of looking at her watch. "And more sexy shoes than anyone I know. But I don't think you're going to have time for a shopping spree, Hay. You're supposed to be picking up the guy in a half hour."

"A half hour!" Aghast that she'd spent so much time dithering over what to wear, she grabbed the next hanger and pulled off her dove gray suit. "Why didn't you say so?"

Sam propped her head in her hand, watching her with amused eyes. As usual, because she wasn't working out, she was wearing her uniform. "Strangely enough, I figured you were still in possession of your typical perception of time. You going to finally sleep with him?"

"Sam!"

Her friend shrugged. "What? It's a valid question."

"I don't intend to sleep with him."

"Ever?"

Busy slipping her pencil skirt up her thighs, Hayley choked on a laugh. "You don't really expect me to answer that, do you?"

"Well, yeah," Sam retorted as if it were obvious. "Gotta live vicariously through someone, don't I?"

"Jane's getting married. You want to envy someone's love life, she's a better bet."

"Hell, no. Married sex? Marriage, period? No thank you." Shuddering comically, Sam pushed off the bed and pulled on the suit jacket, turning this way and that as she stood in front of the mirror. To say it clashed with her dark green uniform was an understatement. But Sam filled out the bust of the jacket better than Hayley did.

Resigned to the fact that she'd never possess the figure with which Sam had been blessed, Hayley returned to the closet to select a blouse. "I know it's a wild theory, but there are *some* who believe that being married to a person you love actually enhances sex." She started to slide the blouse over her head.

"Married people just say that so they'll feel better about what they've sacrificed since the vows." Sam removed the jacket and held it out. "Ditch the blouse," she advised.

"What?"

Sam wagged the jacket. "Bad enough you're wearing a suit. You don't need to button up in a blouse, too."

"I figured we could go to China Palace in Braden. It's the only place around that uses linen tablecloths. But I'll probably know half the people there, so I'm not going without a blouse."

Sam shrugged. "Suit yourself. No pun intended. I'm sure pretty boy will be impressed to go out with a woman dressed for the office." Her wicked smile took away any sting and she pulled open Hayley's bedroom door. "I've gotta get back to the station." She'd only dropped by for a few minutes during her break. "Let me know how it goes."

After she'd shut the door behind her, Hayley looked at herself in the mirror. She did look as if she was heading in for a day of work. The suit and blouse were nearly identical to the ones she'd shed shortly before Sam had showed up. Even adding a pair of multi-strapped black pumps wasn't going to change that fact.

"Sugarnuts," she muttered and whipped the blouse back over her head. She'd twisted her usual ponytail into a low chignon and the pins were already starting to come loose thanks to her hurrying. She didn't want Seth thinking of her as a therapist.

She wanted him thinking of her as a woman.

But she didn't have the nerve to go sans blouse entirely. She found a lacy black camisole that had never seen the light of day—because it was meant to be an *under*garment—and buttoned her jacket up over that. She yanked the pins out of her hair, raked her fingers through it and checked her reflection again.

"You look manic," she told herself and reached for the brush to smooth out her messy hair.

"Hayley, dear." Her grandmother opened

the door, an imperious look in her eye. "Your phone is out here ringing. Shall I answer it for you?"

Hayley tossed the brush on the bed. "I'll get it, Vivian." Addressing her grandmother by her given name was something that made them both more comfortable. Hayley because she'd never met the woman until six months ago. And Vivian because she wasn't fond of being reminded that she was old enough to have several grown grandchildren. Which made little sense, because she'd come to Wyoming to end the estrangement with her family.

"Men like women in dresses, dear." Vivian followed Hayley into the living room. "Once you catch them, *then* wear a suit." The older woman patted the nubby silk one that she herself was wearing. "But until then—" she waved her hand expressively "—wear a dress. Allows them to think they're in charge or something. Men need their delusions."

"I think I'll be fine," Hayley said confidently, despite her own dithering over her clothing, and snatched up her ringing cell phone from the table by the front door. She quickly answered when she saw the number displayed. "This is Dr. Templeton."

"Sorry to bother you at home, ma'am. But you did say to call if he showed any change."

She easily recognized the caller's voice. Which meant the "he" in question was her newest patient, Jason McGregor. "That's all right, Adam. And I did say to call anytime. What's happening? Is he asking for me?" It would be a first. Ever since Tristan Clay requested she take on the case, Jason McGregor had steadfastly refused to interact with her in any meaningful way. That hadn't stopped her from spending several hours each day with him for the past week and a half, however.

"No, ma'am. But he's tearing up his room, so I figured I'd better call."

"He hasn't hurt himself, has he?" Jason's room at the safe house had more amenities than Tristan Clay had initially wanted to provide. She knew her patient was a prisoner. That his quarters were a cell disguised as a modestly comfortable room being monitored every single minute of every single day. It was no different than the military prison where he'd been before Tristan had him transferred into his custody.

And although she might not know the finer ins and outs of what all Tristan and his highly confidential Hollins-Winword actually did—she preferred not to know, actually—she did know that her patient was suspected of having killed his two partners. Tristan was trusting her to either help the man work through his memory loss surrounding the incident, or debunk his condition altogether.

Everyone around Jason seemed to believe he was dangerous. Hayley was still withholding judgment on that. She simply didn't know enough about the man yet.

"He's trying to bang up the place pretty good, but he's not showing any signs of injury," Adam answered.

At least that was something. "I'll be there in ten minutes," she promised and disconnected the call. "A patient," she told her grandmother, who was still standing right beside her.

"Oh, Hayley. What about your *date*?"

To hear Vivian's tone, canceling was akin to dissing the Queen of England. Hayley scrolled through her cell phone history until she found Seth's number. "The date's just going to have to wait," she said as she headed back into the privacy of her bedroom.

Her call was answered after only a few rings. "It's Hayley."

"Chicken out already?" His voice was deep.

"I'm not chickening out." She tucked the thin phone against her shoulder and yanked her hair back into its customary ponytail. "I have a patient emergency."

"Yeah. That's what they all say."

She caught the reflection of her narrowing eyes in the mirror and hastily smoothed out her face as if he could see through the phone to her severe expression. "I don't make up things when it comes to my patients."

"So you make up things when it doesn't?"

"You're toying with me."

"If you unwound a little, you'd be quicker to recognize when a person's joking."

Tension that she hadn't even realized she was feeling released inside her chest. She exhaled and pushed her feet into leather ballet flats. They weren't on her list of favorites, but they were comfortable and no-nonsense and she'd quickly learned that where her newest patient was concerned, no-nonsense was key. In one of his rare verbal offerings, he'd warned her to save both her coddling and her feminine wiles. The fact that she'd offered neither was immaterial. "I *am* sorry, Seth."

"I'll make sure you make it up to me."

"Ha ha. Another joke."

His voice dropped. "No, Doc. That's a promise. Obviously this is going to take some work."

She smiled even though a shiver was dancing down her spine. "I guess we'll see. I'm afraid dinner will probably have to wait until after Casey and Jane's wedding this weekend." She had several group sessions that met during the week in the evenings. And Friday would be busy with the wedding rehearsal and the dinner Casey and Jane were having out at their place. "I don't expect to have any free time until next Sunday at the earliest."

"Guess it will be back to the microwave for me. When I die from malnourishment, drop a flower on my grave."

She laughed softly. "I'll do that. Good night, Seth."

"Good night, Doc."

Still smiling, she slid her phone into the side pocket of her briefcase, which usually doubled as her purse, too, and went back out to the living room.

"All work and no play isn't going to keep you warm at night, dear," her grandmother cautioned.

Even though Hayley felt certain that Vivian hadn't left the house all day except for the morning walk she usually took, her grandmother was still dressed in a Chanel suit with jewels sparkling at her ears and throat. In six months, Hayley had never seen her grandmother dress differently. She seemed to have an endless array of designer clothing and priceless jewelry. Undoubtedly the benefit of having been married once upon a time to a steel magnate. "That's why I have an electric blanket," Hayley assured her grandmother. "Don't wait up. I might be late."

"I wish it were for a different reason." Vivian's acerbic voice followed her out the door.

"Me, too," Hayley murmured as she hurried to her car. "Me, too."

Ten minutes away in the observation room that overlooked McGregor's cell, Seth slid his cell phone into his pocket. Beyond the monitors and the bulletproof glass, the disgraced agent had finally stopped throwing his furniture around and now stood motionless in the middle of the room, staring down at his feet. They were bare below the pale blue medical scrubs that he wore. When it came to acting, the guy was doing a good job of looking as if he was losing his marbles.

Not that his behavior changed Seth's mind at all about McGregor's involvement in his partners' deaths.

He glanced at the young man sitting in front of the monitors. "Thanks for keeping me in the loop, Adam." Strictly speaking, Seth had no official need-to-know where the safe house's "guest" was concerned. But Seth had helped Adam get into Hollins-Winword a while back and loyalty stuck. "Does Dr. Templeton ever check the log?"

Adam shook his head. "I tried showing it to her because Mr. Clay said she was in charge of everything with McGregor except security, but she didn't want to see it. Says her only interest is in her patient. Not the comings and goings of his keepers, since we never interact with the guy."

The only people who did interact with McGregor, according to Adam, were Hayley and, even less frequently, Tristan. Tristan's meetings with McGregor were recorded. Audio and video.

Hayley's, however, were not. She'd evidently dismissed the warnings that being observed during her sessions was for her own safety and insisted that her patient's privacy be honored. Her only concession had been to carry a panic button whenever she was alone with McGregor.

"Well." Seth scrawled the exit time in the log next to his equally indecipherable signature. "Enjoy the grub." He'd brought Adam dinner from one of the diners in town.

"Already am," Adam said around a bite of his roast beef sandwich.

Seth left the safe house and drove his truck well out of sight before pulling to the side of the road. He'd planned to make his usual quick stop at the place to check on things and be home at his apartment in plenty of time before Hayley came. But witnessing McGregor's temper tantrum had waylaid him. And even before he'd heard her voice on the phone, he'd known that Hayley would be canceling on him.

His conscience didn't particularly bother him.

Just because he'd considered the possibility of gaining inside information from her about what McGregor revealed during their private sessions didn't mean Seth was acting on it. She had limited knowledge of those involved with

Hollins-Winword and there was no reason for her to know he was anything other than what she believed him to be: a lowly Cee-Vid security guard.

So he sat there off in the distance on the side of the road and waited until her car arrived. She parked in the driveway of the ordinary-looking ranch-style house situated in the middle of a half-dozen other ordinary-looking houses, got out, walked up the sidewalk and knocked on the front door. A few seconds later, the woman who lived in the house with her real-life husband opened the door as if greeting a friend, and Hayley disappeared inside.

In his mind, Seth followed her movements. Through the living room filled with ordinary furniture. Probably greeting the husband, where he'd be parked on his recliner, watching sports on television after having spent his day in the drugstore where he was the pharmacist. Through the kitchen, which was usually filled with the warm scent of something the pharmacist's stay-at-home wife was baking, and down the stairs to the basement. Then through a steel security door as thick as Seth's thigh and down another flight to the very depths below the house where she'd be greeted by a guard just like Adam who didn't hide the fact that he was armed the way the couple upstairs did.

And even though Hayley had the trust of Tristan Clay, for security purposes she would still have to surrender that sleek briefcase she carried and be wanded and patted down before she'd be allowed into the heavily locked room with her patient, the panic button tucked into her pocket.

The process would take a minimum of five minutes if she didn't stop to shoot the breeze with anyone along the way.

Seth sat there slouched in his truck seat watching the house. Porch lights came on up and down the street as darkness fell and his butt turned numb.

And finally, a little more than three hours later, the front door of the safe house opened again and Hayley appeared on the porch. Accompanied by the lady of the house, she stood there for a moment, smiling and holding a foil-wrapped package in her hand, before returning to her car with a casual wave of her hand.

She definitely had the routine down. Anyone taking the time to watch would have seen only one friend stopping to visit another.

Exhaling, and not particularly anxious to examine the reasons why he was relieved she was out of there, Seth straightened in his seat, started up his ancient truck and drove home to the microwave in his apartment.

"You've got a visitor."

Hayley looked up from her case notes to see

her office manager, Gretchen, standing in the doorway. "Who?"

Gretchen grinned and her eyebrows practically wiggled. "A man."

"Nearly half my practice is made up of men," Hayley replied. But she closed the file folder, slid it into her desk drawer and stood up. She had an hour before her next appointment, which Gretchen—who did her office scheduling—knew very well. So Hayley walked with her to the outer reception area.

The sight of Seth standing there made her breath catch in her chest. She was vaguely aware of Gretchen retreating to her desk behind the reception counter. "Aren't you supposed to be at work?" He was dressed in another black work T-shirt and blue jeans. Common clothes, yet the man wearing them didn't seem common at all.

"Even I get a lunch break." He held up a large brown paper bag. "Think the doctor does, too."

He smiled faintly. "At least that's what I heard from a reliable source."

Hayley looked toward Gretchen. Her office manager was looking down, but she caught the satisfied smile on her face. It seemed Gretchen shared Vivian's opinion that Hayley needed a man.

She looked back at Seth and nodded toward the brown bag. "And that's lunch, I'm assuming. You're obviously well-prepared."

His smile was lazy. "I try to be. Dinner didn't work out last night, but today's a new day. What do you say?" He wagged the bag slightly. "Sandwiches are still warm from Ruby's. Sun's shining and that new park is only five minutes away."

She mockingly narrowed her eyes. "You're trying to tempt me, aren't you?"

"Is it working?"

"I feel that if I admit it is, you'll take advantage of that."

"Scout's honor, I do have taking advantage in mind."

Her breath caught a little all over again. Because he was tempting her. Even more, he was charming her. Yes, she was attracted to him. But she'd never expected the oddly sweet smile lighting his bright blue eyes. And for once, she forgot all about being nervous around him. "Were you ever a Boy Scout?"

"No ma'am. I was an army ranger. Surrender is not a Ranger word." He wagged the bag again. "Turkey pastrami on rye. Won't stay warm forever."

Her mouth watered and she wasn't entirely certain whether it was because of the promise of one of her favorite sandwiches from Ruby's, or because of Seth. "I suppose Gretchen told you I like turkey pastrami."

"I've seen you buy it at Shop-World." He shook his head dolefully. "Don't figure it can hold a candle to the real deal, but I've never seen you buy beef."

"You've noticed what I buy at the grocery store?" Hadn't she done the same where he was concerned?

"I'm an observant guy."

"Stop yammering, Dr. Templeton. If you don't go have lunch with him, *I* will," Gretchen warned. "And since my oldest boy is about his age, I'm sure your young man would be *thrilled*."

Seth just smiled slightly and unfolded the top of the brown bag so that the scent inside escaped even more.

Hayley tossed up her hands as if she hadn't decided she would go with him the very moment he suggested it. "I *have* to be back here by two."

He folded up the top of the bag again. "That's a mission I can handle. Promise."

She chewed back the giddy smile that kept wanting to break free. "Let me just get my purse." She turned, hurried back to her office and grabbed her briefcase. She glanced at the decorative mirror on her office wall and barely stopped herself from fussing with her appearance.

She'd passed out pretty much at his feet the night she'd gone home with him. It was safe to say he'd seen her at her worst, and she was dressed the same way she always was when she came to the office. Ponytail. Suit.

Still, she pinched the apples of her cheeks to rosy them up before she returned to the reception area. When she got there, he had his elbows propped on the high counter and was talking with Gretchen. Hayley barely had enough time to drag her eyes away from the perfect fit of denim over his perfect rear when he straightened and turned toward her.

And judging by the amusement in his eyes, she wasn't sure she'd been fast enough.

"Ready?"

She swallowed, trying not to examine too

closely the feelings swirling around inside her. Because sometimes a woman had to follow her instincts and just go with the moment.

"I'm ready," she answered. Was she ever.

Chapter Four

The name of the new park was, indeed, Willow Park. Obviously in honor of the stand of young willow trees planted on one side. There were also a couple stands of cottonwoods and a lot of grass that hadn't yet filled in.

"You're right when you said we wouldn't run into anyone here," Hayley observed as Seth opened her door after parking in the small parking lot and walking around the car. "There isn't another vehicle here."

"Give it time." He took the bag, which she'd

held on her lap during the short drive, and gestured at the buildings under construction across the street. She could hear an occasional whir of power tools and hammers. "When those houses are finished and people start moving in, the place'll probably be crawling with kids."

She smiled and followed him to the winding sidewalk that led from the parking lot, past the sandy playground, to one of the picnic tables positioned under the ramada. The weather was still cool and she was glad for her suit jacket against the breeze that was strong enough to make the swing set chains jangle musically. "Judging by your tone, I'm guessing you don't have any. Kids, that is."

"No. No kids. No exes down in Texas." He glanced at her and gestured for her to sit. "Or anywhere else for that matter. I'd pull out the bench for you but it's attached to the table."

She couldn't lift her foot over the bench to sit without hitching her skirt up her thighs, so she sat first and then rotated, swinging both her legs over the bench till she was facing the table. Then she felt like a ninny when she caught his grin as he took the bench across from her. "What?"

"Never appreciated quite this much what a straight skirt did for a pretty girl." He set the bag on the table between them.

Warmth filled her cheeks, which needed no help from pinching this time. She quickly pulled open the paper sack to extract the contents. Not only were there two wrapped sandwiches that were still slightly warm, but also an insulated container of coleslaw, two bottles of water, two brownies and a ridiculous quantity of paper napkins.

She held them up in her hand. "Emptied the dispenser, did you?"

"I've seen how dangerous you are when it comes to water."

"Don't remind me." She unfolded one of the napkins and set the sandwiched marked "TP" on it. “That night at Colbys was definitely not one of my finer moments.” She didn’t particularly want to talk about it, either, but pretending it hadn’t happened was pointless. “Is that where you’re from? Texas?”

He didn’t bother using a napkin as a placemat the way she did. Just unfolded the foil-backed paper from his sandwich and nodded before taking a healthy bite.

“Texas is a big state.” She unwrapped her own sandwich, savoring the scent that greeted her. “Whereabouts?”

He swallowed and opened one of the water bottles. “Little bit outside Dallas.”

“Your parents still there?”

“No.” The answer was short and didn’t invite further queries. “You’re not from Weaver.”

“How do you know that?”

“The night you went home with me, you kept saying you were supposed to be home in Braden.”

Ouch. "I don't remember that. Did, uh, did I say anything else?" Any other little nuggets that would prove humiliating, right along with the way she'd passed out? She took a bite of her sandwich to make sure she didn't actually voice that thought out loud.

"Just that you hadn't had sex in a long time."

She nearly choked on her food.

He uncapped the second water bottle and held it out to her, his eyes full of laughter. She looked past him at the empty playground equipment, the swings swaying softly, and drank down a third of the bottle before setting it down next to her sandwich. "How long have you been out of the army?"

"Pretty quick change of subject there."

"I think it's best," she managed to say.

"Five years."

She grimaced. "I told you that, too?"

"Since I left the rangers. But I guess I don't have to ask you just *how* long is a long time."

Mortified, she tried not to squirm. “And now you can understand why that is. I love Ruby’s coleslaw.” She grabbed the container that had been weighing down the spare napkins. Several napkins immediately flew off the table with the breeze.

He chuckled and lifted his hand. “Relax. I’ll get ’em. Don’t want your friend from the sheriff’s department writing us up for littering.”

While he retrieved the fluttering paper squares, she tucked the rest of the napkins safely back inside the bag and silently told herself to get a grip. Then she realized that there was only one plastic fork.

She was fitting the lid back on the container when Seth returned. “Thought you loved Ruby’s coleslaw,” he said.

She lifted the lone fork. “Only one of these in the bag.”

He sat back down and gave her a look. “Then use it,” he drawled as if it were obvious.

Feeling as if she'd already embarrassed herself enough, she silently took the round tub and peeled back the lid again. The coleslaw was as delicious as ever, but her enthusiasm for it had definitely dwindled and after several bites, she set the fork back down.

He was having no such problems with his appetite, though, and was working his way steadily through his sandwich. She could see that it was crammed with thin slices of roast beef and not much else, unlike her sandwich that had lettuce, tomatoes and peppers in addition to the turkey pastrami. "Texas is even more cattle country than Wyoming, I guess."

"We do like our beef. But you don't seem to touch it at all. Don't meet many folks around here who share your tastes."

She lifted her shoulder. "My father blames it on my mother. Says I inherited it from her. She didn't eat meat at all. She was from Cheyenne and was doing a college tour in Pennsylvania when they met. They married a week later."

"Fast work."

"Whirlwind romance. Instead of becoming an engineering student, she became an army wife."

"Which made you an army brat."

"Not for long. Dad stayed in only until I was three. Archer—my older brother—and I were both born in St. Robert, Missouri."

"Your dad was posted at Fort Leonard Wood?"

She nodded. "Have you been there?"

"Few times." He'd finished his sandwich, so he balled up the wrapper and stuck it in the bag before reaching across the table for the coleslaw and fork. "What happened when you were three?"

She raised her eyebrows, trying not to think anything of the way he scooped up a forkful of the shredded cabbage and placed his lips around the same fork she had. "Who says anything happened?"

"Your face."

She shook herself a little. The way she kept getting physically distracted by him was unnerving in the extreme. It was one thing when she was three sheets to the wind. Another when she was sitting in a park with nothing inebriating in her system at all except him. "My mother died that year."

He slowly lowered the fork, a frown pulling his dark brows together. "That's rough."

"Even when you are only three." She smiled sadly. "Except through pictures, I can't really remember her face. But I can still recall the way she'd read me stories at night before bed. The way she smelled when she hugged me." She exhaled. "Anyway, with two young children and no family of his own in the area—none he wanted to see, anyway," she amended, thinking of Vivian, "he decided to take us to Cheyenne."

"Where your mother had kin."

"Right. Plus my uncle had already moved to

Braden by then. He's still a pediatrician there." And just as unhappy now as her father was when it came to Vivian's continued presence in Wyoming.

"So why the hop from Cheyenne to Braden for your dad?"

She smiled. "That would be Meredith. My stepmother. She's from Braden. They got married when I was six."

"Three years. That's pretty quick."

"But not as quick as with my mother. Meredith's wonderful, though. She's my mom in every way that matters." Nor did she treat Hayley as if she'd done the unforgiveable by taking in Vivian. Meredith kept trying on her end to soften Hayley's father's rigid stance.

"They have any more kids?"

"Triplet girls." Hayley grinned at the thought of her three half sisters. "They're identical but they couldn't be more different in personality if they tried. And before marrying my dad, Mom had already had Rosalind. So there are actually six of us kids."

"One big, happy family."

"Happy is a relative term," she replied. "Archer and Rosalind have always been at odds. Becoming adults hasn't really changed that. But ultimately, among all of us, 'yours-mine-and-ours—'" she air-quoted the phrase "—we're pretty close." Her siblings couldn't care less that Vivian had come to town. Even though Hayley's parents and aunt and uncle had refused to attend Hayley's Christmas Eve get-together, her brother and the triplets had come and had gone away with their own impressions, content to leave the family dissension in Hayley's lap. "What about you? Any brothers and sisters?"

"Just me and my pop."

It was more than he had offered before, and though she was curious about his mother, she contained herself from asking about her. "What prompted you to go into the army?"

"Same thing that prompted your dad to get out. Death." He looked over his shoulder at the softly jangling swings. "When's the last time you were on one of those?"

She was used to bouncing around from topic to topic with her patients, so his abrupt shift didn't unduly throw her. "I can't even remember," she admitted with a faint laugh. "I'm not sure I played much on the swings or the slides even when I was a child. I was more the studious type. Always had my nose in one book or another. You?"

"Broke my arm jumping off a swing set when I was seven."

"Somehow, I am not surprised."

He raised one eyebrow.

"You seem the adventurous type."

"Well, I liked sports," he allowed. "Adventure tends to have a price. Learned that after fifteen years in the army. Reason I got out. Got tired of fighting a battle that I'd finally realized was unwinnable."

She had the distinct sense that the battle he meant hadn't been a military or political one. But he didn't give her an opening to pursue the subject further. "You going to finish that here," he nodded toward her sandwich, "or take it back with you?" He'd already polished off the remainder of the coleslaw.

She shook her head. "This is my favorite sandwich. Only thing I like better from Ruby's are the cinnamon rolls. But as a leftover, I am happy to pass. You want it?" She nudged it toward him.

Considering his seemingly endless appetite, she wasn't surprised when he didn't hesitate to finish it off in a few bites. "Guess we're running out of time, Doc."

She felt only too aware of it, but instead of packing up, she impetuously swung her legs back over the bench again and stood, nudging her skirt smooth again. "We'll come back and clean up in a few minutes," she said as she started across the sidewalk toward the playground. When she reached the sand that softened the landing area around the swings, she removed her shoes, left them on the cement and continued on barefoot. "Come on."

"It was just a question, Doc." His voice was lazy and amused. "Not a suggestion."

"I know." She wrapped her hands around the chains of one of the swings and sat down on the rubber seat. "You were changing the subject. A tactic I've been known to use myself, as you know." Stretching out one leg, she pushed off slightly with the other. "Come over here anyway." She tilted her head toward the other unoccupied swings. "Shame that the only thing moving these around right now is the breeze."

He unwrapped one of the brownies before standing and crossing over to sit on the swing beside her. He downed half the brownie in two bites. "You're never quite what I expect."

She wasn't swinging high at all, but she was still surprised by the exhilaration she felt. "Spilling food, ruining shirts and passing out drunker than a skunk?" She made a face. "Not very appropriate for the town shrink, I'm afraid."

"Psychologist," he corrected dryly and she couldn't help but smile. "So why *were* you drunk?"

She tilted her face upward toward the sun and closed her eyes. The warmth felt good on her face. "That is a conversation for another day, I think. Would take too much time."

"And your two o'clock will be waiting soon."

"Yes." She heard a soft jangle of chains but didn't open her eyes until her backward arc was caught mid-swing, halting her motion abruptly. Startled, she looked up to see Seth standing behind her. "What are you doing?"

"What I've wanted to do for a long time." He

leaned over her head from behind and brushed her mouth with his.

She'd barely inhaled the surprise of it along with the taste of chocolate on his lips when he straightened again and gave her a strong push that sent her swing flying three times as high as her modest efforts had. The sound that came out of her throat was half screech and half laugh. "Seth!"

He was already crossing back to the picnic table where he collected their debris and deposited it in one of the metal trash bins. Then, after gathering up her unfinished bottle of water and the remaining brownie, he returned to stand on the sidewalk in front of her. "I have a promise to keep."

She'd never once been reluctant to do the job that she loved. But she was reluctant now. "Am I going to shock you if I admit I don't really want to go back?"

He smiled slightly. "No. All work and no play

isn't good for anyone. You're a shrink. You probably preach balance—" he drew out the word mockingly "—to all the crazies who lay on your couch."

She did talk about balance with her patients who clearly didn't possess it. And she tried not to think about the irony, when her own life was heavily skewed toward work. But she didn't want to talk about that now, so she leaned forward, her ponytail sliding over her shoulder as she swung away from him again. "No 'crazies,' as you so indelicately put it. Nor do I have a couch in my office."

"Neither do I."

Which served to remind her that she wasn't the only one on a lunch break. And whereas she was her own boss, he was not. So when the swing scooped forward and back again, she let her toes drag through the sand, slowing the motion enough that she could jump off. And when she stumbled forward, she wasn't surprised at all that he was right there to catch her before she fell. But as soon as she was steady, his hand dropped from her shoulder and he held out the brownie to her.

Exhilaration was still flowing in her veins as she took the plastic-wrapped treat. "You seem very tall," she admitted breathlessly. She was five-seven and he had a good half foot on her.

His eyes crinkled. "You seem very short," he returned and bent over to pick up her shoes. He dangled them in front of her. "Without these."

"I'm still not short," she countered and took them from him. She set the pumps upright on the sidewalk and slid her feet back into them, which brought her eyes considerably closer to his. Instead of making her feel more in control, though, it just made her more aware of how close the added height brought their lips.

"My sisters, now," she said quickly, "*are* short." She briskly set off for the parking lot and silently noted the way her fingers had squeezed the brownie from a perfectly cut rectangle into a near bow-tie shape. “The Trips, I mean. They’re five-two if they stretch. Which is an inch more than their mom.” He’d left the door unlocked, so she pulled open the squeaking passenger door and quickly tucked the brownie out of sight in a side pocket of her briefcase. She hadn’t been worried about her belongings. The truck had been in full sight the entire time, and there wasn’t a soul around except them anyway.

Stepping up onto the running board, she pulled herself up into the high seat and fastened her seatbelt while he got behind the wheel. Only then did she reach for her cell phone, also inside her briefcase.

Seeing she had four missed calls from Tristan Clay had her grimacing. There was only one reason he’d call her directly, and that was because of Jason McGregor.

“Something wrong?”

“Don’t know.” She unclicked her seatbelt again.

"Would you mind waiting for a moment?" She didn't really wait for an answer as she pushed open the door and climbed back out again, moving a few feet away from the truck before listening to the only message that had been left.

Seth watched her from inside the truck. He hadn't seen the display on her phone so had no way of knowing who or what had put the serious look back in her eyes. Could be a patient. Could be McGregor for all he knew. Or it could be something more personal.

At the moment, he was just sorry to see that the lighthearted smile inside her chocolate-warm eyes had departed.

When she looked at her phone and tapped the screen before holding it to her ear again, moving even farther away from the truck, he decided it was a patient. A few minutes later, she ended her call and returned to the truck, her lips set.

"You all right?"

"Yes. A small crisis, I'm afraid." She chewed her lip and seemed to come to an abrupt decision as she looked at him. "With a…a friend. Would you mind dropping me at her house? She lives closer to here than if I went back to the office to get my own car. I'm sure you have to get back to Cee-Vid—"

He backed out of the parking spot. "Where's her house?"

Hayley's lips and eyes both softened slightly. "Turn left at the end of the block. She lives in that new development out past Shop-World. Toward Cee-Vid's airstrip. I assume you know where that is?"

His hands tightened fractionally around the steering wheel. The safe house was in the general direction she described. "I do. I'm surprised that you do." Not many people did.

She exhaled, as if relieved. "Last year, Mr. Clay loaned one of his Cee-Vid planes to Casey so that he could take Jane to a funeral. She told me about it." She refastened her seatbelt while she called Gretchen and asked her to reschedule the rest of her appointments for the afternoon.

Even though Hayley held the cell phone tightly to her ear, Seth could hear the laugh in her secretary's voice as she said, "My, my. Lunch went that well, did it? I have never been happier to reschedule Mrs. Pittman."

Hayley's gaze skittered over him. Her cheeks were pink. From the sun, possibly, but he'd already seen for himself the way she could blush. For a woman whose profession was delving into the minds and emotions of others, it was a curiosity to him that she could still blush at all.

"It's not like that," he heard her mutter into the phone. "I'll check in with you in a half hour. Thanks, Gretchen." Then she was tucking the phone back in the side pocket of her briefcase. "Sorry."

"Why?"

"Because—" She broke off and shook her

head. "It doesn't matter." She pointed out the turn ahead. "Left there."

And a few minutes later, it was a right. Then another left.

The closer they got to the safe house, the tighter Seth's nerves got. For all he knew, she *could* have a friend living out this way.

But the prickling at the base of his neck was telling him otherwise.

And when she gestured vaguely a few minutes later and said he could just stop on the street and drop her off, he knew his instinct had been right on the money. "You need me to wait?"

She looked genuinely surprised. "Oh, no. You've done enough already." She gathered the strap of her briefcase and pushed open the door. "I don't want to keep you any longer than I already have."

"It's not a problem. I have an understanding boss in Mr. Clay." He hoped to hell she would never know how ironic those words were.

Her cheeks looked even brighter. “My friend can get me back. Thanks, though. And thanks for lunch, Seth. I really enjoyed it.”

“So did I.” The words were true. So much more than they should have been, considering the situation.

She looked over her shoulder at the quiet house and then back at him. “I’m still holding you to dinner. After everything calms down.” She pushed a blond lock of hair that had come down from her ponytail back behind her ear. “With the wedding and all.”

And all, he figured, included McGregor. “Sure. Maybe I’ll even see you at the wedding. You can save a dance for me at the reception.”

A shy smile bloomed on her lips. “I’d really like that.” Then, seeming to realize that she was just standing there smiling at him, she quickly shut the door and headed briskly up the walk toward the front door of the safe house.

He was pretty sure the chaos surrounding

Casey and Jane's wedding would be well over long before things were resolved with Hayley's "patient."

And he was even more certain that when it came to Hayley and him, Seth wasn't going to be able to wait that long. Not now that he'd tasted her lips again. And no dance at a wedding reception attended by half the town was going to suffice.

He waited until she reached the front door, which opened the second that she got to it. Without a backward glance, she disappeared inside and the door closed once again.

He pinched the pain between his eyebrows and turned the truck around, driving back the way he'd come.

He'd barely pulled into the Cee-Vid parking lot when his own phone rang. He pulled it out of his pocket and let out a long, low curse at the sight of "Boss" on the screen. Reluctantly, he put the phone to his ear. "Yeah?"

"What the hell do you think you are doing?"

He sighed. The pain between his eyebrows deepened. "You were at the house," he surmised.

"And saw you drop off Dr. Templeton." Tristan's voice was terse. "I want an explanation."

Rather than enter the Cee-Vid building, Seth veered off to one side where he could speak without being overheard. "She had a crisis with a 'friend.' Her words. I dropped her off." His boss's silence spoke volumes. "We had lunch together," Seth finally added.

"Why?" It wasn't curiosity in the other man's tone; it was demand.

Seth rubbed his hand down his bristled cheek. Even though he had spent fifteen years answering orders in the army, he'd spent the past five happy to remove that from his daily routine. Right along with looking like a clean-cut recruiting poster model.

But Tristan was still his boss. And Seth had

no desire for that to change. He didn't like the situation with McGregor, but he understood the need for the Hollins-Winwords of the world. So he answered.

"Because I like her," he admitted. "She has no idea that I know what's going on inside that house."

"You want McGregor's hide nailed to a wall," Tristan countered. "You could never prove your father's partner killed him, but you're damn sure going to make sure McGregor doesn't get away with killing your friends."

Seth sucked down the emotion that rose hot and quick inside him. He'd been too young and green to do anything about it when the authorities had decided that Chuck Banyon's drowning on a boating trip with his business partner had been only a tragic accident. That the business deal they'd been at odds over hadn't been adequate motive.

But that had been two decades ago. And despite knowing he'd failed to unearth the truth, Seth was no longer a devastated kid. "Because I *like* her," he repeated tightly.

"Then *un*like her," his boss said flatly, "or be damned certain that her appeal has absolutely nothing to do with the fact that she's the only one McGregor is talking to. I don't want anything messing up this case, and that includes you messing with Dr. Templeton!"

Chapter Five

"Vivian." Hayley maintained a calm tone despite the frustration building inside her. "You *promised* you'd go with me to the wedding tomorrow."

Vivian's diminutive figure was wrapped in a heavy gold silk robe. But even dressed as she was for bed, she still had a long strand of pearls around her neck. She was working them between her fingers as if they were worry beads as she paced across Hayley's small living room. "You're going to be busy, dear. I haven't been a maid of honor since the Stone Age, but I do remember it is a busy time. The styles may have changed, but I highly doubt that has."

Hayley sank down on a chair and toed off the shoes that she'd been wearing for the past several hours, all through Casey and Jane's wedding rehearsal and the dinner they'd thrown at their place afterward. It was late. And on top of a nearly full day at work before that, it felt even later. She wanted sleep. She wanted someone to put their arms around her and solve the world's problems.

Who was she kidding?

Problems were what *she* was supposed to be good at solving.

She wanted Seth to put his arms around her, period.

But Seth wasn't here. She hadn't seen or talked to him since he'd surprised her with lunch three days earlier.

And her grandmother *was* here. "When's the

last time you were out of the house? Besides your morning walk?"

Vivian's lips tightened. She was eighty-six years old but the same dark brown eyes that Hayley also possessed still held plenty of life, and right now they clearly broadcast her displeasure. "If you want me to leave, Hayley, you need only say the words." She sniffed haughtily. "You wouldn't be the first family member to wish me gone, after all."

"I don't wish you gone, Vivian," Hayley said quietly. Honestly. "You surely know that by now."

Her grandmother sighed heavily, some of the starch leaving her rigid posture. She crossed to the couch and sat in the corner, looking smaller than ever and unusually delicate. "You've been hospitable for six months."

"It's not hospitality driving me," Hayley corrected. "You're family. Maybe if you'd just tell me what happened between you and my father and Uncle David, I could—"

"They're unforgiving souls," Vivian said abruptly. "That's what happened." Her lips tightened again. "They're not at all like their father. He forgave anything, even when doing so proved ruinous."

Hayley's bed was so close, yet further away than ever. "Tell me more about what he was like. My grandfather." Vivian had already told her how they'd met. She'd been a violin-maker's daughter and Sawyer had been a rich young man who'd played the violin. "Besides the fact that he played violin."

"Rich," Vivian said so immediately that Hayley couldn't help but smile even as tired as she was.

She propped a pillow behind her back and crossed her bare feet on top of the coffee table. Vivian had had three husbands after Sawyer

Templeton, but she'd never taken their names. Only Sawyer's. "And?"

"And handsome. And…he had a soft heart." Vivian's pearls clicked softly between her fretting fingers. "Too soft, I always thought. Particularly for a young man inheriting a steel empire. I thought I was the strong one."

"Women often are," Hayley murmured.

"I wasn't strong, though. I was just typical. A product of a privileged life. Which I'd had, even though the Archers were nothing like the Templetons." Vivian suddenly pinned her with a look. "Times were different then, Hayley. When I was a young woman. You understand that, don't you? Reputations. Scandals. They could ruin a person back then."

"Some might say they can ruin a person now. But, yes, I understand what you're saying." She just wished her grandmother would be more specific about what had threatened to ruin Sawyer

Templeton. It was hard to untie a knot if all you knew was the general length of the rope.

"There were *expectations* of people like your grandfather. And his father before him. There were things one did. And things that one simply did not do. People of our class didn't mix with… others." Vivian made a face. "And yes, I know how that sounds. But back then…" Her voice trailed off and she looked away. "I was nineteen when I married Sawyer," she said after a moment. "He was four years older. I believed that the only thing of importance was fulfilling all of those expectations. But Sawyer… Oh, he was just different. He didn't care what other people thought. So it was up to me to care."

"Vivian," Hayley prompted gently. "You were a young woman in a different time. Nobody here is judging you for anything, except you."

The pearl clicking got faster. "Now I'm paying the price."

"My father and Uncle David will come

around." Saying the words helped to remind Hayley, too, that there was always hope they would at least attempt some sort of reconciliation with their estranged mother.

Vivian's expression was tight. "They wouldn't accept the photograph albums I put together as Christmas gifts. The albums you said would have some impact."

"And I still think it would make an impression that you'd preserved so many memories from their childhoods." She'd put the carefully wrapped boxes containing the albums in her closet so Vivian wouldn't be constantly reminded of them.

"Yet Carter wouldn't even come here on Christmas Eve to see his own daughter because I was here," Vivian said. "He's more like *me* than he ever was like his father. Unforgiving to the end."

"Well, the end isn't here yet," Hayley countered immediately. "I'll try talking to Dad again.

Remember, you've only been in Wyoming for six months. That's not a lot of time, considering how long it's been since he and Uncle David both chose to leave Pennsylvania."

Vivian finally released her pearls, rested her head against the couch cushion, closed her eyes and sighed. "Thatcher left first," she murmured. "My firstborn. He broke my heart. And then he died in that horrible skiing accident and I never had a chance to tell him I loved him."

"Vivian." Hayley moved from her chair to sit beside her grandmother and gently took her beringed hand in hers. "You will still have time to tell your family that you love them."

Vivian slowly opened her eyes and stared at the ceiling. "I'm an old woman. I don't have forever to wait, dear. I'm closer to the end than I want to think about."

Hayley wasn't going to deny the basic fact of her grandmother's age. "The same thing can be said of any of us. Life is never a given—not for anyone, regardless of their age. The fact that Thatcher died when he was a young man is proof of that. So the point is to act while you can.

"Maybe we haven't gotten through to my father and Uncle David yet. But *please* don't let that stop you from getting out there and living your life right now. You have to stop hiding yourself here in my house. I know how different Weaver is from what you're used to. But I can count on one hand the number of times you've gotten out and about with me. The only thing you do is walk around the block each morning. Do you stop to say hello to anyone?"

"You don't understand."

Hayley squeezed Vivian's hand. "Then help me understand."

"You're very much like my dear Arthur," Vivian murmured.

Hayley knew that Arthur Finley had been the last of her grandmother's four husbands. That before his death, he'd been the one to encourage her to mend the long-standing rift between her and her sons. "I would have liked to have known him. I'd like to think my dad and Uncle David would have, too."

"They would have just accused me of causing his death, too," Vivian said tiredly. She finally looked at Hayley. "That's what they always blamed me for. Driving Sawyer to his suicide."

Hayley absorbed that, trying not to show her shock.

Not once had she ever heard her father say anything about the death of his father. "Arthur died of cancer. You told me that months ago. They can't very well blame that on you. And suicide is—"

"Sawyer did *not* commit suicide," Vivian said flatly. "He died in an automobile accident when your father was only a baby. Sawyer was terribly upset with *me* as usual, but he never would have abandoned his children, no matter what they grew up to believe."

"How would they have even gotten the idea of suicide?"

"Because Thatcher was convinced. When he was sixteen, he found the accident report. It had never been made public. The benefits of wealth and influence." The soft lines in her face seemed even more prominent. "Sawyer's car ran off an embankment. The cause behind that was never established. But Thatcher drew his own youthful conclusions."

Vivian had once run through her litany of husbands and Hayley quickly calculated. "Was this before or after your second husband died?"

"Just after Theodore died." Vivian's lips twisted. "Thatcher was hardly upset about *that*. He'd never gotten along with Theodore and certainly didn't grieve his death. I can't blame him for that, though. I hardly got along with Theodore. Our marriage was mostly convenience. I had three young sons. I needed a husband to help raise them, and he was suitable. And he liked marrying into the Templeton money."

"Whether Thatcher liked him or not, Theodore was still a father figure for your sons. Grieving or not, his death undoubtedly affected Thatcher, too. As well as his brothers. Teen years are impressionable ones."

Vivian didn't respond to that, instead choosing to return to the subject of Jane and Casey's wedding. "You should have a proper date for the wedding tomorrow."

"I have a proper date." Hayley lifted Vivian's hand and lightly kissed the back of it. Because she'd learned more details about Vivian's life when her dad was a child in the past ten minutes than in the entirety of her grandmother's six-month stay, Hayley knew better than to push Vivian where she didn't yet want to go. So she rose to her feet and gave her grandmother a steady look. "And I'm expecting her not to stand me up. For one thing, I would very much like a chance to introduce her to more of my friends." She hesitated, and then dangled some actual bait. "One in particular."

Vivian eyed her. "The young man who surprised you with lunch even after you'd cancelled your dinner date?"

Hayley nodded. She was too adult to acknowledge the giddy curl inside her, but that didn't stop it from happening. "Seth knows Casey from Cee-Vid. He'll be at the wedding." And the reception, though she didn't bring herself to offer up that piece of information. A comment about saving a dance was one thing. Actually having it come to pass was another. "If you really do want to meet him, it will be a good opportunity."

Vivian pursed her lips. "You're pretty good at maneuvering people where you want them."

Hayley's eyebrows shot up and she let out a dismissive laugh. "If only, Vivian. I would be having a much easier time not just with my family, but with some of my patients." She leaned over and picked up her discarded shoes. "The wedding's not until four. I'll be coming and going for most of the morning, but I'll be here to get you at three. Agreed?"

Vivian let out a put-upon sigh. "Fine." She slowly pushed herself off the couch and the diamonds on her hand winked in the lamplight. "I know it wouldn't be white tie at that hour, but will a cocktail dress suffice?"

Hayley nearly chewed her tongue in half to keep from laughing because her grandmother was obviously serious. "Um, sure," she managed. If Vivian had spent more time getting to know some people around town, she never would have had to ask the question. Around Weaver, jeans were de rigueur, even at a wedding. "But anything you would wear to church would be just fine, too," she assured her grandmother. Frankly, the clothes that Vivian wore every day around the house were more formal than what most of the local guests would undoubtedly be wearing. “You’re going to be fine, no matter what, Vivian. Trust me.”

“And what about you? Did you finally get your dress from the seamstress?”

“Isabella Clay,” Hayley confirmed. Casey’s cousin-in-law had made the dresses for the wedding party, including the bride’s. “I managed to get over to her place this afternoon to pick it up.”

“And?”

“It’s lovely.” Isabella had once been a costume designer for a ballet company in New York. And Hayley had gotten to know her when she’d been counseling her now-adopted son, Murphy. “Even you will approve. Come on.” She took her grandmother’s hand. “I’ll show you. And you can help me decide what I need to do with my hair.”

The pleasure on Vivian’s face was worth putting off going to bed for a little while longer.

Seth stood outside the Weaver Community Church, watching people file through the open front door to attend Casey and Jane's wedding. The last time he'd worn a tie had been with his dress uniform before he'd left the rangers, and the pale silver one he wore now felt confining. He kept wanting to tug it loose, but a lifetime of self-discipline kept him from doing so.

The wedding was supposed to start at four and it was nearly that now. He and Casey had spent a lot of long hours together inside the cavernous communications center hidden away in the center of the Cee-Vid building where they watched over the safety of Hollins-Winword agents and assets all around the world. Casey had invited him to the wedding, so Seth had agreed. But he couldn't say he'd had any burning desire to actually go rub elbows with the couple.

No. The draw now wasn't his buddy the groom or the bride. It was the maid of honor. Which in turn was the reason why going inside the church was now a problem.

He was an invited guest and had a reasonable

excuse for being there. But he'd also been essentially warned away from Hayley by his boss.

He'd spent the past four days arguing with himself over that call from Tristan. Assuring himself that his interest in Hayley wasn't increasing exponentially because of her interactions with McGregor.

He was pretty sure it wasn't.

But he knew himself. As a ranger, he'd always gone a hundred and ten percent above the call to succeed. Working with Hollins-Winword wasn't any different. He believed in justice, and at times getting there wasn't a pretty thing.

Which left just enough room for doubt about his motives that it made his neck itch worse than the damn tie.

Hayley Templeton was an ethical woman. She wasn't going to tell him anything about what went on in her sessions with any of her patients.

Except she was starting to trust him. Or she

never would have had him drop her off at the home of her distressed "friend."

Still, she wouldn't tell him anything about what went on in her sessions. Not intentionally.

He muttered an oath that inside the church would probably have had the roof caving in on him and turned around to head back to his truck. He'd had to park down the street because the small lot alongside the church was already overflowing. He yanked the tie loose as he went.

By the time he was driving away, the church doors had been pulled shut. He figured that probably meant that the ceremony was about to begin. Hayley would be occupied. It wasn't likely that she'd even notice his absence among that crowd, crammed inside and breaking every occupancy limit law there was.

Because Casey was related to practically half the town's law keepers, Seth doubted there'd be any complaints lodged on that particular score.

He would have stopped at Colbys for a beer,

except the place was closed up tight so Jane's employees could go to the wedding and reception. Ruby's was closed, too. Not that they served alcohol over there anyway. There were a handful of other places in town he could have gone, but he passed them all by, too, and finally found himself back at Cee-Vid.

Nobody was working at that hour on a Saturday. He made his way unimpeded through the cubicles of the game design floor and back to the security office, where he entered his security code, which allowed entrance to Control through a well-hidden door in the wall. Once inside the communications center, he encountered other Hollins-Winword personnel.

Clay family wedding or not, guardians would always be on watch over Hollins-Winword's best in the field. He grunted acknowledgment of the handful of preoccupied greetings he received and sat down in his usual seat in front of a bank of computer screens spread across the wall. But he didn't log into the system. There was no point because, like it or not, his head was still back at the church, imagining Hayley inside.

It was a helluva thing to face the fact that when he was with her, he couldn't get rid of the thought of work. And when he was at work, he couldn't get rid of thoughts of her. Maybe the two areas of his life could have coexisted just fine if not for one thing: McGregor's so-called amnesia.

He pinched the knot in his brow, pushed his chair back and propped his heels on the edge of the console in front of him.

And there, despite the occasional, curious comments he got from the others, he stayed for the next several hours. Until he was certain that there'd be no chance of having that dance he'd told Hayley to save.

"I haven't seen pretty boy here." Sam plopped down on the chair next to Hayley with a flutter of taupe-colored tulle and silk charmeuse and handed her one of the champagne flutes she was carrying. "Weren't you expecting him?"

Hayley shrugged, trying not to let her disappointment show. "He probably had to work or something." She sipped the champagne and watched the dancers on the portable floor that had been set up beneath the huge white tent. It didn't matter that the dinner had been served, the cake cut, the toasts made. Even though the bride and groom had already left the party—as had a good number of guests, including Jane's sister, who'd been the third bridesmaid—the entire place was still crowded with people celebrating.

There weren't many locations in Weaver equipped to handle such a sizeable wedding reception, so Jane and Casey had created their own venue on the expansive property just outside of town that was owned by Casey's sister and brother-in-law. In deference to the evening chill, propane heaters burned in several locations, and they, along with the heat from the guests themselves, were doing an admirable job of keeping the tented area cozy. So cozy that neither Sam nor Hayley had had to use the wraps that Isabella had created to go with their tea-length gowns.

"Sorry," Sam murmured quietly. "I know you were looking forward to seeing him, Hay."

"I was." There was no point in pretending otherwise. "But things happen. I'm sure he had a reason." She took another small sip of champagne. "I also wish my grandmother would have come to the reception. Even she would have been impressed with the setup here. Not a single detail's been missed."

Sam nodded, looking around the tent's elegantly appointed interior. "At least Vivian made it to the wedding," she said. "I saw her sitting next to Sloan and Abby."

"For a while. I thought she'd be more comfortable sitting with them." Abby was an old schoolmate of Hayley's cousin from Braden. She'd recently married Sloan McCray, who worked with Sam at the sheriff's department. "She just wasn't comfortable enough to stay very long. She claims she has a headache, but—" She waved her hand. "You know Abby's a nurse. She and Sloan were kind enough to drive Vivian back home for me. She said Vivian seemed agitated at the church, but once they left, she calmed down and was fine when they dropped her off. I don't know if the headache is real, or if it's just another one of Vivian's excuses. When she first came to town, she wanted to know who everyone was and what they were doing."

"I remember." Sam started to prop her ankle on her knee but then thought better of it, tugging with some annoyance at the fluff of skirt billowing out around her slender ankles. "When you introduced us to her at the harvest festival after Halloween last year, she was all about getting clued in to who, what and where. I remember thinking she would fit right into Weaver—even if she does go around wearing fancy clothes—as long as she likes gossip."

"Of which Weaver has plenty," Hayley finished. "She was interested at first. But she's been getting more and more reclusive. Particularly the past few months. We talked a lot last night and I thought we were making progress."

"You did. She came to the wedding. Crimminy. Everyone was there. Even Jane's ex-husband came." Sam bumped her shoulder against Hayley's. "Talk about a hottie. Casey's a good-looking guy, but Gage Stanton?" Sam fanned herself, smiling wickedly. "I could think of a few wonderfully naughty things to do with him."

"Tall, dark and handsome does it for you?"

"Tall, rich and temporary does it for me," Sam countered with a laugh. "Jane says he's a workaholic and so am I. It's a match made in hottie heaven."

"Except you live here and he lives in Colorado."

"Details shmetails," Sam countered dismissively. "I hear the advantage of all that money is that silly little problems like that are easily solved."

"You wouldn't sleep with Jane's ex-husband," Hayley scolded. "And you know it."

"Yeah." Sam's lips curled. Her hair was several shades darker blond than Hayley's. She usually wore it in a no-nonsense, shoulder-length bob, but this evening, it surrounded her head in a tumble of soft waves that she kept pushing impatiently away from her face. "S'pose you're right. I'm surprised Casey wasn't bugged by Gage coming, though. He's Jane's *ex*. A little weird, if you ask me."

"Vivian thought it was unseemly. She told me so when I called a little while ago to check up on her. I told her the same thing I'll tell you—Casey's not threatened by Jane's past, and she's not threatened by his. They're adults who trust each other and who've made a commitment to each other, and that's where their focus rightfully is."

"How *adult* of you," Sam drawled. "If my man's ex came sniffing around at my wedding, I'd want to scratch out her eyes."

Hayley muffled a laugh. "Nobody's sniffing around anyone, Sam."

"More's the pity." Sam polished off the rest of her champagne and stood. "I'm going for more before they run out. You?"

Hayley shook her head as she held up her flute that was still more than half full.

"Lightweight," Sam accused with a smile and turned to make her way across the tented area to the bar set up on the other side.

Hayley stood, too, but only to circle around to the table where a pile of wedding gifts had collected over the course of the evening. She was housesitting for Jane and Casey while they were on their honeymoon, so she'd told them that she'd cart the items back to their place. They could open them when they returned from Europe in a few weeks. She selected two of the largest presents and carried them out of the tent to her car, which was parked nearby, thanks to the organization of J.D.

It wasn't long before she had help. Soon the gift table was cleared and Hayley's little sedan was jammed. Back inside the tent, Sam was on the dance floor, champagne glass in one hand as she danced with one of Casey's cousins. Hayley was one of very few left who didn't possess the name of Clay, and because it was pretty much only family members who were still hanging on, Hayley figured it was okay if she left.

She retrieved her wrap from where she'd left it at the head table, fastened the sparkly glass button that held it together in front and quickly made the rounds for goodbyes. She returned to her car and got in, gathering up the voluminous layers of finely woven sheer fabric around her legs so she could get the door closed.

When she'd spoken earlier with Vivian, Hayley had promised to bring home some aspirin for her after the reception. It wasn't really late yet, not even ten o'clock, according to the DJ on the radio. But the only place in town open on a Saturday evening was Shop-World. Fortunately, the big-box store was on her way home.

When she walked through the brightly lit entrance a little while later, she decided that the convenience almost made up for traipsing through the place dressed in taupe-colored froth.

She found the aspirin, remembered they needed coffee and a few other items, and exited the store a half-hour later pushing a cart with a noisy wheel and several bulging bags.

"All dressed up and nowhere to go but Shop-World?"

She stopped short just outside the exit, the squeaking wheel going mercifully silent, and felt a tangle of emotions at the sight of Seth. He was heading into the store that she was so quickly leaving. "My grandmother needed some aspirin." Without benefit of propane heaters and an encompassing tent, the night was cold and she shivered beneath her wrap. "This place was on my way."

"I'm sorry I didn't make it." He wore dark jeans and a jacket open down the front enough that she could see a white shirt beneath. Not his typical black T-shirt at all.

"It's too bad." She was absolutely mortified to feel her throat tightening with tears and wished she could just chalk it up to an overfull day. "It was a really nice party," she managed. "Everyone seemed to enjoy it." Even she had managed to keep up a front of enjoyment over the disappointment swamping her when she'd realized he wasn't coming.

She shivered again and started gathering up the handles of the plastic bags inside her cart.

Easier to carry them than listen to the racket of that noisy wheel. And escaping quickly was becoming paramount.

"Hayley."

"I need to get this aspirin to Vivian," she said abruptly. "She had to leave early because of a headache." Hayley was developing one, too. Every pin holding her chignon in place seemed to be digging through to her brain.

She lifted the bags from the cart and turned hurriedly toward the parking lot, where she'd left her car beneath one of the tall, beaming lights. Her dressy, high-heeled shoes provided no comfort at all as she quickly walked away from Seth. Even as used to wearing heels as she was, her feet were screaming at her.

She heard his footsteps behind her, providing a whisper of a warning before she felt his hand catch her arm from behind.

"Hayley."

She turned faster than she realized and the

weight of her purchases whipped around, too, knocking right into him before the thin plastic split and seven pounds of coffee beans landed at their feet, exploding in a shower of aromatic shrapnel.

Chapter Six

"Dammit!" Hayley stared down as the beans showered to the ground, immediately followed by the plastic bottle containing her grandmother's aspirin and an industrial-sized box of tampons.

"What happened to *sugarnuts*?"

The tears had worked their way from Hayley's throat to the backs of her eyes and she blinked hard. She adjusted her hold on the remaining bags so she wouldn't drop them and crouched to grab the box of tampons. "Unless you plan to wash my mouth out with soap, I think I'm safe," she said thickly. She shoved the box out of sight inside one of the other bags and looked around for the aspirin bottle that was the sole reason she'd stopped at the store in the first place. She didn't see it anywhere.

His hands slid under her arms and he gently lifted her. "Your dress'll get dirty spreading out like that all over the ground."

"Fortunately, I never have to wear it again." The waspish words escaped as she found herself standing once more. She sent a silent apology to Isabella for the slight against the lovely dress and didn't look at him as she shook one foot to dislodge the coffee beans that had snuck between her toes.

"That'd be a shame, considering how pretty you look. Why are you shaking your foot like that?"

She immediately stopped, even though there was still a hard little bead underneath the ball of her foot. She realized he'd somehow maneuvered the remaining bags out of her hands.

"It's dark outside." Her voice was flat. "You have no idea how I look."

He caught her elbow with his free hand and steered her the last several feet toward the circle of yellow light shining down around her car. "I know enough. You have your keys, I assume?"

She managed not to cringe as she turned away from him and pulled the key fob out from where she'd tucked it down the front of her strapless gown.

Her attempt at subtlety obviously had failed, though he said nothing more than a low "hmm" when she brushed past him to unlock the car door. The second she pulled it open and the interior light came on, she realized her next problem.

With all the gifts packed inside, there was barely enough room for *her* to get in, much less add the contents of her four surviving grocery bags. “Oh, for cryin’ out loud.”

He tilted his head at an angle as he studied the dilemma. “Trunk just as bad?”

In answer, she hit the button, and the trunk lid popped open. He moved around to the back of the car and blew out a low whistle.

“I’ll figure it out.” That seemed to be the lifelong pursuit she’d chosen, after all. Figuring it all out. And if she weren’t still so…so…hurt that he’d been a no-show, she wouldn’t be bothered by that fact at all. Instead, even though he’d never made her any promises, she felt like a teenaged girl who’d been stood up for the prom. “Just leave the bags on the ground,” she finished, her voice flat.

He gave her a look.

She huffed and gathered the wrap more closely around her shoulders.

“At least start up the car and get the heater

going," he suggested in a reasonable tone that grated on her nerves. "I'll do some rearranging."

"I don't need your—" She pressed her lips together on the unvoiced "help" when he gave her another long look. "Fine." Tossing out her hands, she got into the car, started up the engine and flipped on the heater.

Even though she'd been in the store for only half an hour, all the heater did was blow out air just as cold as that outside the opened car door. It would take several minutes before it started to warm. She fished the last coffee bean from her shoe, then got out of the car and headed back toward the area where she'd dropped the bags, hoping to find the bottle of aspirin so she wouldn't have to make another trip inside the store.

The only thing she wanted to do was crawl into bed, pull the covers over her head and get the day over with so she could start fresh again tomorrow. When she worked with her female clients who felt that way, she informally referred to it as having a "Scarlett moment." Everyone had their metaphorical Tara. A breathing space. A haven to lick wounds and plan for a better time.

She was no different.

She heard him close her trunk as she walked in a widening circle around the coffee graveyard, peering down for a glimpse of the small white bottle among the smattering of cars parked nearby.

"It's cold." Seth joined her and settled his jacket over her shoulders, right on top of the thin wrap. "Tell me what you're looking for and I'll find it."

She'd automatically grasped the sides of his leather jacket as the warmth it still bore, heady and full of a promise she knew better than to trust, encompassed her. "The aspirin bottle." Her voice was husky. "I should go back in and buy another."

"I'll find the bottle," he said again and gently

pushed her in the direction of the car. "Go sit in your car and get warm."

Because the tears were burning again, she did what he said. Huddled in the worn-soft jacket that smelled like him, she fitted her voluminous skirt around her legs again and pulled the car door closed.

She rested her forehead on the steering wheel and exhaled slowly. Inhaled slowly.

She focused on the feel of the car engine rumbling smoothly underneath her, the heater vents finally blowing out some warmth and Blake Shelton's deep voice crooning sweet nothings from the radio. By the time Seth rapped his knuckles on the window beside her, she'd cobbled her composure together once again.

She lifted her head and rolled down the window so he could pass her the found aspirin bottle.

"It rolled behind someone's tire," he said.

"Thanks." She started to roll up the window

once more but he closed his fingers over the top of it, stopping her.

"I wanted to be there."

She dragged her eyes away from the tips of his long fingers so close to her face and ran her thumb back and forth over the inside ridges on the bottom of her steering wheel.

She could and would hold on to the calm she'd regained.

"You don't have to explain."

He propped his arm on the top of the car and leaned down so he could see better into the car. "I feel like I need to. I had some stuff inside my head I was trying to work out."

To a psychologist's ear, the line was pretty unimaginative. She tucked her tongue behind her teeth for a moment and gave him a sideways look. "And did you work it out?"

His lips twisted. "Wish I could say I had, but—" He broke off and shook his head. Then he softly thumped his hand against the top of the car. "Would've liked to have had that dance," he said with an odd finality and straightened. "Be careful driving home, Doc."

He turned and started walking away, his white shirt looking ghostly in the dark.

She realized then that she was still wearing his jacket, and she quickly got back out of the car. "Seth!" Leaving the car running, she hurried after him, holding out his jacket. "You forgot this."

He reached out and his hand brushed hers as he slowly took the coat from her.

She started to pull away, but his fingers followed and tangled with hers.

She went still on the outside, but on the inside all of her hard-won calm dispersed like dandelion fluff in the wind. Her blood suddenly rushed through her veins and she looked at him, wishing that she could see his expression.

But it was much, much too dark.

Then he shook his head a little. "Sugarnuts,"

he muttered and dropped his jacket on the ground as he stepped closer, sliding his arms around her beneath her wrap, tightening his hold until their bodies were suddenly flush.

Her knees went weak and a shaking breath leaked past her lips. "Seth—"

"Shh." His lips brushed her temple. "Just listen."

The only thing she could hear was her pulse throbbing inside her head. Or maybe it was his.

But after a moment that felt endless, she finally realized that his feet had begun moving slowly in time to the faint music coming from her car radio.

Warmth swept through her chest, spreading ever outward until she forgot everything around them as they danced to the song. Then to another. And another, right there on the dwindling edge of light cast by the light fixture near her car.

And he didn't stop. Not until headlights swept over them as a car passed nearby.

Only then did he finally step away.

He folded her hand around his arm and escorted her back to her waiting car. He tucked her dress around her legs when she sat down in the driver's seat, and without another word, he gently closed the door between them and walked away.

Aching inside, Hayley watched him go.

He didn't head toward the brightly lit store.

He just disappeared into the darkness.

The DJ on her radio was talking, but his words might as well have been gibberish and she turned it off. The air coming out of the heater vents was hot, and she turned that off, as well.

Then she wiped the moisture from her cheeks, fastened her safety belt and drove home.

Vivian was sound asleep on the couch. Hayley left the aspirin bottle on the coffee table where her grandmother would be sure to see it when she woke. Then she soundlessly went into her bedroom, leaned back against the closed door and pressed her hand flat against her heart.

It was still there, right inside her chest. She could feel it beating.

Which seemed odd considering Seth had stolen it from her in the parking lot at Shop-World.

Two days later, Hayley walked into the subterranean room that Jason McGregor had taken to calling "Home, Sweet Home." He'd even scratched out the words on the wall above the two-way mirror that Hayley insisted be deactivated during their sessions.

"Good afternoon, Jason." She didn't usually carry a notepad into their meetings, but she had one with her today. She set it on the small shelf alongside the side chair where she made herself comfortable. Jason was sitting on the bed across the room with his back against the wall. He was barefoot as usual, and today, he'd also shunned his loose-fitting cotton shirt.

Which left the array of old, faded scars criss-crossing his chest and arms on display.

She didn't comment on them, though, instead focusing on the splint on his hand and wrist. "How is your hand feeling today?"

"Like I punched it through the wall last week." His voice was flat and he didn't look at her. "I want some books to read."

It had been just over two weeks since she'd first met him, but this was the first time he'd asked anything of her. She considered it a huge step forward, though she hid her surprised relief. "Anything in particular?"

"Fiction."

"Are there authors that you prefer?"

"Don't care. Figure getting my head in a book is the only way I'm gonna get outta here."

"Okay." She glanced at the tray of food sitting on a small chest of drawers that, along with the bed and her chair, made up the room's sparse furnishings. He'd already reduced a desk to splinters and torn to shreds a second chair during one of his fits of temper. They hadn't been replaced. "Doesn't look like you've eaten much of your lunch."

"Why do you keep coming here every day?"

"Why do you suppose?" She waited a beat. "Because I'm the eternal optimist. And it's my job to help you."

His eyes finally shifted to her. The expression in them was as flat as it always was. "Help the crazy guy remember that he killed his partners?"

She didn't flinch. He wasn't a fool. He knew what he was suspected of having done even though there was still no actual evidence. Tristan had admitted that if it weren't for the government's involvement, they wouldn't have been able to keep him in custody for this long. Not when they couldn't establish a motive, and the only evidence he'd been involved in his partners' deaths was circumstantial. But Tristan was also convinced Jason was better off under his watch than the government's. "Did you kill them?"

"How should I know?" He finally showed some emotion, shoving his fingers through his unkempt hair and pushing off the bed to pace around the room. He was pale and too thin; the blue drawstring pants hung on his hips. "The only freaking thing I remember is my name."

He grimaced and swore even more viciously. "What I thought was my name." He gestured at the mirror and the people he still believed were watching their sessions even though Hayley had assured him otherwise many times. "They're the ones who told me it's really Jason."

All of this she also knew. She uncrossed her ankles and set her notepad on her lap. "I'd like to try something new, if you're willing." She reached into the side pocket of her slacks, her fingertips brushing over the panic button as she extracted the short pencil that, along with the notebook, was all she'd been allowed to bring in with her. Jason wasn't even allowed plastic eating utensils at this point because he was far too adept at causing damage with even the most innocent of objects.

He wasn't suicidal. But he definitely had bouts of rage. Considering everything he'd been going through for the past several months, even those fits probably stemmed from reasonable cause.

"Hypnosis," she finished.

He snorted and returned to sit on the bed with his back against the wall, his long legs crossed. "Doesn't work."

"How do you know?" She'd spent enough time with him now to feel confident that his condition wasn't an act. He truly did not remember anything. Physical causes for his amnesia had already been ruled out before he'd been placed under Tristan's "care." Which left the psychological. He could very well have been involved in the death of his partners, but if so, she honestly believed he couldn't recall the memory. "Do you remember?" she asked with a faint smile.

He bared his teeth in a humorless grimace. "Don't quit your day job, Doc. You're no good at standup comedy."

Doc. Too easily, Seth snuck back into her mind.

She stared hard at the blank pad she'd put in her lap until his image was once more pushed behind the barrier that separated her personal life from her professional.

"Hypnosis," she continued calmly, "can be a very useful tool in recovering dissociated and repressed memories. But it's nothing that can be forced on you, Jason. Not by me or anyone else. You have to be willing to participate. To try."

"And when I do remember, I spend the rest of my life on death row. Or worse," he added with a look toward the mirror.

"We don't know that yet."

His expression was skeptical to say the least.

"My plan isn't to work on that right now," Hayley continued. "Your entire life isn't made up only with the time you spent in Central America. You had parents. Siblings. A childhood. You went to school. To college." All of these things she knew from Tristan. But Jason couldn't recall any of the details. "Let's just start with retrieving memories from your childhood. When you learned you liked reading fiction, for instance," she added. "Or we can spend another hour together twiddling our thumbs again." She spread her hands slightly. The man was a prisoner. He needed to feel some control, particularly when it came to his own mind. "Your call."

He thumped his head against the wall behind him a few times. "You went to a wedding this weekend," he said abruptly. "I heard the gorillas talking."

The work–life barrier in her head vibrated a

little but held fast. "There was a wedding. A lot of people went."

"You're not married."

"So we're going to talk about me today?" She shifted and crossed her ankles again. "No. I am not married."

"Gay?"

If he'd hoped for a reaction, he would be disappointed. "Unmarried. I like to read thrillers," she mused smoothly. "Political intrigue. An occasional love story."

"I think I was married," he said abruptly. "Once."

Ah. She wanted to cheer but contained it to an encouraging smile and set aside the notepad. "I'd like to hear about that, Jason."

She was walking the dog.

More accurately, the dog was walking Hayley, practically dragging her along by the long leash she held as they crossed the street and entered the big community park.

For the past two days, ever since he'd unintentionally run into her at Shop-World, Seth had been telling himself that staying away from Dr. Hayley Templeton was the smart thing to do.

But what was a man to do when the universe put her in his orbit?

His rhythmic pace didn't falter at the sight of her. Which meant it took only minutes for their paths to cross near the pavilion. Just when she was depositing a plastic bag into the trash with quite an expression on her face.

"Looks like you're on doody duty," he greeted as he slowed to a walk. The park was a hive of activity even on an early Monday evening. There was even a group of little girls dressed in tutus twirling around under the pavilion to the clapping of their dance instructor. "Fun times."

Hayley dropped the trash bin lid back into

place and eyed him as if he'd materialized out of nowhere. "What are you doing here?"

"Same thing I do most every day after work. Five miles." Then there was the shooting range, followed by the dinky gym at his apartment building. He absently pulled the front of his sweaty T-shirt up to swipe his face with it, only realizing what he was doing when her gaze followed the movement.

She looked fresh-faced and feminine and he was an uncouth, sweating beast.

He let go of the fabric and went down on one knee to scrub his fingers over the dog's yellow coat. "Isn't this Casey's pup? The one that keeps eating his shoes?"

"Moose," Hayley provided. "And not just shoes." She'd pulled a tiny bottle of hand sanitizer from the back pocket of the blue jeans that accentuated her long legs and squirted some onto her hands.

He couldn't keep from chuckling over the

sight. She'd probably want to shower in the stuff if he pulled her close the way every cell in his body urged.

"*What*?" She pocketed the bottle again. "I'm not big on doody duty, as you call it." She folded her arms over the front of the long-sleeved thermal shirt that clung to her slender torso. Moose's enthusiastic bouncing around tugged the end of the leash clasped in her fingers, which in turn made her arms bounce around, too.

And every time her arms bounced, her breasts plumped distractingly beneath the close-fitting top.

"At least he hasn't tried eating any of my shoes," she continued. "Not that I've given him a chance. I keep them in the closed guestroom closet. Which doesn't stop him from chewing instead on the edge of the closet door and most anything else he can get his teeth around. I'm staying at their place while they're on their honeymoon," she added. "I thought I'd try tiring him out some with a long walk, to see if he'd sleep more and chew less tonight." Her gaze shied away from Seth's and she moistened her lips. "I was, um, going to stop at Colbys and grab a sandwich for supper after I walked Moose. I still owe you dinner for that shirt. If...if you're interested."

Looking up at her provided him with a new perspective. She had a tiny birthmark underneath her slightly pointed chin that he'd never noticed before.

He gave the slobbering pup a final pat and stood up. Between the bouncing arms and that cute little mole he wanted to kiss in the worst way, he was too close to heading off a cliff. "You don't owe me anything, Hayley."

"In other words, thanks, but no thanks." She took a steadying step when the dog jerked hard on the leash. "Moose, stop." Of course, the words had no effect and the dog kept prancing around until he'd twisted the leash around Hayley's ankles. Not that she seemed to notice. "I got into psychology because I was always interested in what made people tick. But I can't figure you out at all."

"There's nothing to figure."

The fine line of her jaw was firmly set as she looked past him. "So I'm just…imagining this *thing* between us." The corners of her soft lips turned downward. "A little humiliating, but I'll survive. Come on, Moose." She started to step around Seth, only to learn what he had already noticed about the leash. She nearly stumbled into him.

He caught her easily but let her go the second she was steady again. "Stand still for a minute." He worked the twisted leash free of first her fingers and then her ankles. It was one of those retractable types and before giving the handle back to her, he hit the button to shorten the leash by several feet. "Don't give him the advantage of such a long lead," he suggested.

"You know." She folded her arms beneath her breasts again. "The only time I'm a klutz is when you're around."

"Why do you suppose that is?"

She made a face. "That's my line. Not yours. Enjoy the rest of your run." She didn't smile as she turned and tugged, trying to draw the dog's attention from the bush he was sniffing. "Moose! Come *on*."

The puppy finally turned and loped along ahead of her, a disjointed collection of body parts going at different speeds, all covered in thick, yellow fur. In a matter of minutes, she was leaving the park and crossing the street again.

So much for the long walk for Moose.

Seth blew out a breath and forced himself to turn and go the opposite way. He still had a few miles to run before he'd hit his quota.

A part of him wished he'd never heard of Hollins-Winword, Tristan Clay or the dinky town of Weaver, Wyoming, where a person couldn't seem to turn around without running into someone they needed to avoid.

If he hadn't, his life would have been so much simpler.

He picked up his pace, returning to the familiar, rhythmic thump, thump, thump of path underfoot.

And if he hadn't, his life—thump, thump, thump—would have been missing the increasingly vital element that was Hayley Templeton.

Chapter Seven

After leaving the park, Hayley did not pass Colbys.

She did not pass go or collect two hundred dollars.

Running into Seth that way just made her want to head home and lick her wounds. But she couldn't even do that. She was staying at Jane and Casey's, taking care of their wrecking-ball-in-training of a dog, Moose.

Even though Hayley hadn't stayed at the park long thanks to that wholly unsatisfying encounter with Seth, the entire trip still had managed to eat up more than an hour of time. As she walked up the stone drive leading to the white, two-story farmhouse that Casey had transplanted to its present neighborhood, she let Moose off the leash. He raced with all the speed and none of the grace of a greyhound across the green grass surrounding the house and up the wooden steps of the front porch, skidding headfirst right into the door.

She heard his yelp, but because she'd already witnessed similar scenes before, she wasn't unduly concerned. By the time she reached the porch, Moose was sitting on his haunches, a goofy smile on his face while his wagging tail thumped against the door. "You're such a silly boy," she murmured, scratching his head before letting him through the front door.

She walked through to the fully renovated gourmet kitchen and great room located at the rear of the house and refilled the dog's water bowl before opening the oversize refrigerator. The glass shelves inside were spotless and mostly empty. Jane had made noises about getting it stocked for Hayley before she and Casey left for their honeymoon, but Hayley had assured her not to worry about it. Between preparing for the wedding and taking care of Colbys, the last thing the new bride needed to be worrying about was laying in food for her house sitter.

Hayley needed to get to the store.

But ever since running into Seth outside of Shop-World after the wedding, she hadn't been able to bring herself to go back and stock up on her usual items. And the small, local grocer in town had been closed both times she'd thought to run by.

She closed the fridge doors and dialed her house number. Vivian answered on the second ring. "Want me to come home and fix you dinner?" At least there the refrigerator had a few items in it besides leftover wedding cake, Casey's beer and Jane's favorite chardonnay.

But even in this, Hayley was thwarted when her grandmother replied, "I've already eaten."

Hayley leaned against the granite-topped island that seemed the size of a helicopter pad. "When? Today?"

"Don't take that tone with me, miss." Vivian's own tone was haughty. "If you must know, I ordered in."

Hayley nearly laughed out loud. "You ordered pizza?" Because that was pretty much the only option in a town where the sole Golden Arches was still in the planning stage. To say there was a dearth of takeout in Weaver was an understatement.

"I hired Mr. Bumble to cook for me."

Hayley pressed her fingertip to the bridge of her nose. "Who's Mr. Bumble?"

"That young man who works at Ruby's. He has

that dreadful haircut and never wears a proper shirt. But he makes a lovely quiche."

It took Hayley a minute. "You mean Bubba?"

"I refuse to address anyone as *Bubba*," Vivian answered. "Mr. Bumble has agreed to prepare a proper dinner for me for the next week until Montrose arrives."

"Vivian." Hayley pulled out one of the barstools tucked beneath the kitchen island and sat down. "I know I can be preoccupied sometimes, but who is Montrose? And since when have you been getting over to Ruby's to even know what sort of quiche Bubba's capable of making?"

"You told me to get out," Vivian said crisply. "I got out. Don't start complaining now."

"I'm not complaining," Hayley quickly assured her. "Everyone is just full of surprises today."

"Who is everyone?"

She couldn't very well talk about Jason McGregor's bout of loquaciousness that afternoon. And broaching the subject of Seth would just set her grandmother off on another you-need-a-man tangent.

So she didn't address the question at all. "Who is Montrose?" she asked again instead.

"My chef from Pittsburgh. Well. He used to be my chef, before I let him and the rest of the household staff go last year. Of course he'll decide that he needs hazard pay once he sees the state of your small kitchen, but that's temporary and he's always been a prima donna."

Maybe Hayley needed more protein in her diet because she was having the hardest time keeping up. "If you were worried about meals, you could have just said so, Vivian. I thought you were looking forward to having the place to yourself for these few weeks while I'm house sitting."

"I was. But I've decided it's time to move on."

Dismay squeezed inside her. "You're going back to Pennsylvania?"

"Why on earth would I go there when I've already gone to some trouble convincing Montrose to come *here*? I had to actually apologize to the man for having let him go. Really, Hayley dear. For an intelligent young woman, you're very illogical."

"Gee. Thanks." She propped her elbow on the countertop and rested her forehead on her hand. "Then what did you mean by moving on?"

"I've decided I'm no longer going to worry about Carter and David. Dear Arthur, rest his soul, convinced me to try, and I did. I failed. So be it. Time to move on."

"Vivian—"

"No. There is no point in sugarcoating this any longer. I've thought about what you said the other night, and you were right. It's time I start living my life again."

"I applaud proactive behavior, Vivian. But I'm not ready yet to give up on Dad and Uncle David."

"That's up to you. In the meantime, I've decided to buy us a house. A suitable house. Not just a little cottage like you have."

Hayley hesitated, more internal alarms going off. "Us."

"Mr. Bumble provided me the name of a Realtor in town. I will make an appointment to begin looking as soon as possible. Of course, we'll need accommodations for Montrose. He's always lived in, and I expect that won't change."

"Vivian."

"So Montrose and a housekeeper. Housekeeping is beneath him, naturally. And acreage would be nice." Vivian's voice went dry. "I'm assuming there isn't a lack of that in the area."

"Vivian!"

"Yes, dear?"

"Why would you assume I want to move?"

"Why wouldn't you? With a large enough house, we won't even have to see one another if we choose not to. Mercy. I once spent half a year living with Theodore without having to exchange two words with the man. Not that I'm comparing you to Theodore, mind you. I'm simply trying to make my point."

"I like my house," Hayley said.

"Hmm. Well, it's cozy. But you might as well become accustomed to certain things, Hayley. I have no one else to leave my money to—Carter and David would probably spit on every dollar and your siblings and cousins don't give me the time of day—so you're going to be a very, very wealthy woman one day."

"If you want a relationship with my brother and sisters or our cousins, you could make an effort, too. And I don't care about your money. I care about you."

"And *I* care about where we live," Vivian retorted as if that were that. "Now, I can't sit here talking on the phone all evening with you. I have plans to make. Was there anything else you needed?"

Hayley shook her head, feeling as if she'd walked into some alternate universe. "No."

"Then I'll be in touch tomorrow. Good night, dear."

The line went dead.

Hayley slowly set down her phone and looked at the puppy. "Who was that masked woman, Moose?"

The dog just cocked his head, one floppy ear folded backward. Bemused, she bent down and righted his ear, scratched his belly a few times when he immediately rolled over begging for it and then returned to the refrigerator.

Vivian might have "Mr. Bumble" cooking personal meals for her, but Hayley was still left with a lot of empty shelves.

She pulled out the bakery box sitting on the bottom one and cut herself a thick slice of leftover wedding cake. Then she poured herself a glass of chardonnay from the half-empty bottle stuck inside the refrigerator door.

"I know," she told Moose as he followed her out of the kitchen, water dripping off his muzzle onto the gray-stained wood floor. "I'm going to regret it when morning comes. But some days just call for extreme measures."

She carried her wholly inappropriate dinner out to the front porch and sat in one of the two old-fashioned rocking chairs.

The house she rented and that Vivian had evidently deemed unsuitable wasn't far. Just a few circuitous blocks away. Vivian would learn quickly enough that available housing in Weaver generally didn't allow for much choosiness. That was one of the reasons there was so much new construction going on at the other end of town.

Out where Seth lives.

She mentally lined up the whispering voice inside her head, threw a dart and imagined a punctured balloon spewing air as it spun around until spent.

The sun was heading toward the horizon.

She propped the heels of her tennis shoes on the other rocker and watched the colors bloom as she sipped on her wine and plowed her way through the velvety chocolate cake with salted caramel filling. No such thing as an ordinary white cake for Jane and Casey. They both loved chocolate, so chocolate they had served. When her plate was empty, she set it on the porch rail out of Moose's reach. He'd fallen asleep beside her chair, but she wasn't taking chances where he was concerned. Then she sat back again and cradled the wineglass against her midriff while the sunset slowly faded.

"You look like you're ready to fall asleep."

She jerked her feet off the other chair and gave Moose an accusing look. "Some watchdog you are."

The dog's eyes didn't open. His snoring didn't cease.

Not even when Seth came up onto the porch and stepped right over the canine.

Seth still wore his running gear: loose black gym shorts and a dull green T-shirt with the arms ripped out. Neither of which did a bit of good hiding his sinewy muscles.

Realizing she was staring, she looked away and took a fortifying gulp of wine that emptied the glass. "What are you doing here, Seth?"

He held up his hand, revealing a paper sack that she hadn't noticed while she'd been busy ogling his bod. "You've probably replaced it by now, but just in case."

She didn't want to know what he'd brought. Undoubtedly, it would be something that would send her right back down the track of the emotional rollercoaster that she was on where he was concerned.

When she didn't reach for the bag, she heard him sigh a little. He pulled out the package of her favorite brand of coffee beans, set it next to her empty plate on the porch rail and turned to go.

She ground her molars together. She was not going to go after him.

She was *not*.

"Sugarnuts," she muttered and pushed off the rocking chair. "Seth. Just… Oh, for cryin' out loud." She sounded exactly as grumpy as she felt and didn't care. "I seriously do not know why this has to feel so complicated," she said when she reached him. Before she let herself think—and talk herself out of it—she pulled his head down toward hers and pressed her mouth to his.

Exhilaration shot through her veins when his hand went immediately behind her neck, his lips moving hungrily against hers. "I shouldn't be doing this," he muttered.

"Then you shouldn't have come here." She didn't care that they were in full view of any neighbor who cared to look. "You said you had no exes. I know you don't have a wife here. I'd have heard about her by now."

"No wife anywhere." His hand slid from her neck down her spine, fingertips kneading.

"You were all set for this three and a half months ago," she reminded and went back to his lips. Sank her fingers in his hair. The thick strands were tangled. Slightly damp. And heaven help her, she was reveling in it.

"Hayley—" His hands slid to her hips and she felt his resistance.

"I might have had some wine," she added, "but I'm not in danger of passing out this time."

He broke the kiss and then pressed his forehead against hers while holding her hips at bay. "I didn't think you were."

Her breath was fast. "Then what's the problem? What's so different now from the night you took me home from Colbys?"

"McGregor." His voice was low. Flat.

It was the very furthest possible response from her mind, and she was certain she couldn't have heard right. "What?"

Seth's wide shoulders lifted and fell. He pulled his hands from her and took a step back. "McGregor," he repeated.

She felt everything around them—the man two houses down tinkering with his car in his driveway, the woman across the street pushing a stroller, the breeze rustling a set of nearby wind chimes—fade into a single pinpoint where Seth was the center. "What do you know about him?" Her own voice sounded hollow in her head.

"I know if you don't stop it, he's going to get away with killing his partners."

She rubbed her tongue against the sharp edge of her teeth, attempting to drag her hormones back under control while trying to figure how on earth she could respond.

Excluding Tristan Clay and the guards at the safe house, Hayley could count on one hand the number of people around Weaver who she knew for certain were involved with Hollins-Winword. Tristan's nephew, Axel, and his niece, who was married to the sheriff, were local. Hayley had also done some counseling with three other individuals, none of whom lived right there in Weaver at all. Tristan had flown her to work with them in Seattle for two weeks.

That had been nearly two years ago.

Seth was still watching her silently. Her fingers still carried the feel of his thick, dark hair.

She curled them into her palms and folded her arms. "Who do you work for?"

"Who do you think?"

She exhaled. "I think we'd better take this inside." She turned on her heel and returned to the house, snapping her fingers to draw Moose's attention. She carried the empty plate and wineglass back to the kitchen and heard the front door close.

A moment later, Seth walked into the kitchen, too.

"You're not really a security guard," she said.

"No."

"And you work for Tristan Clay."

"Yes."

"Why didn't you tell me before now?"

"There was no reason for you to know."

"And there is now?"

"Eleven years ago, Manuel Rodriguez, Jonathan Solomon and I served together in a joint operation. They were—"

"—Marine recon," she finished for him. "I read their files." Along with Jason's. "Everything that hadn't been redacted, anyway." She set the wineglass down on the counter and decided it was the perfect time to empty the bottle into it. Fortunately, considering the way she couldn't make her hand stop shaking, there wasn't a lot of wine left.

"They were good men. And a little more than six months ago during an operation in Central America that had been years in the making, they were betrayed. By their own partner. By McGregor."

"You have proof of that?"

His blue eyes narrowed. "The only proof that matters is he's alive. They're not."

"Not exactly an ironclad case, or he'd have been charged by now."

He planted his palms flat on the gleaming granite island. "Lying about his memory buys him time. He's guilty."

Her patient could very well be guilty. She couldn't deny that. But she didn't believe he was lying. "And me? How long have you known about my involvement?"

"Since the party out at Tristan and Hope's."

Everything inside her sank.

That had been just over two weeks ago. The very first day she'd met with Jason.

It felt so much longer.

"So *that's* what the supposedly renewed interest in me was about," she murmured. She lifted the wineglass and drank down the remaining mouthful.

It tasted like vinegar.

"You could have just asked me outright what Jason has been telling me during our sessions together." She could barely bring herself to look at him. "I wouldn't have told you then, either, but at least it would have saved you some trouble."

"There's nothing *supposed* about my interest in you." His voice was flat. "I knew you wouldn't tell me squat. Not intentionally."

"Not unintentionally, either," she said tightly. "Sorry to burst your bubble, Seth, but not even in the throes of passion would I have broken a patient's confidentiality." Anger dripped from her words.

"You had me drop you off at the safe house where he's located. Because you were starting to trust me."

"God forbid. Trusting someone to drop me off at the home of a *friend*."

"Tristan saw us."

Her jaw was so tight it hurt. "So? If you'd have

been the Cee-Vid security guard you claimed to be, why would that matter?"

"I'm not a security guard. I'm an intelligence analyst with Hollins-Winword *and* I have a history with the victims. Having a relationship with the psychologist in charge of the number-one suspect in their murder isn't exactly smiled upon. The hint of something compromising like that could blow the case out of the water before there was even the slightest chance of getting it in front of a judge. And that's only if we don't lose McGregor to the Feds first!"

Her chest squeezed. "We don't have a relationship."

His eyes sharpened. "You sure about that?"

Her mouth felt arid. She turned away from his too-sharp gaze and rinsed the glass under the faucet with soap before turning it upside down on a dishtowel to dry. "We aren't dating. We haven't even—" she struggled to push the rest of the words out "—slept together. We are not in a relationship."

He threw her words back at her. "This *thing* between us that is not in your imagination tells me otherwise."

She finally turned back around to face him. "Seth—"

His expression was tight. "I need to stay away from you. Until this business with McGregor is over. I need to stay away from you, for everyone's sake. Even McGregor's."

She swallowed the knot in her throat. She was shaking from her head to her toes. "Then stay away."

A muscle in his jaw flexed. "Believe me," he said. "I have tried." He slowly moved around the island until he stopped in front of her, trapping her in the corner where she stood near the sink.

She couldn't seem to look away from his blue, blue eyes.

"And I can't," he finished in a low voice.

Her lips parted.

His head dipped toward hers, his lips grazing hers, lighter than his whisper. “Don’t trust me, Hayley. Be stronger than I am.”

A sound she didn’t recognize slid from her throat. Her hands curled into fists, one against the counter and the other on the cool edge of the old-fashioned apron sink. The front of her felt singed by the heat emanating from him. “I’m not strong.”

His lips rested against hers and his palms covered her fists. His fingers circled her wrists. Then he lifted and placed her hands on his shoulders and she didn’t resist. “You have to be.” Then he lifted her by the waist, bringing her mouth up to his level. “You have to be,” he repeated and kissed her.

Her mind exploded in color. She instinctively wrapped her legs around his hips, thinking that she’d be anything he needed her to be as long as he never stopped kissing her.

"Where's your room?"

She twined her arms around his back and tasted the hard line of his jaw. Salty and rough with bristle. "Upstairs. First door on the left."

She expected him to put her down. But he just turned, sliding one arm beneath her rear and carried her.

She pressed her face to his neck. If she hadn't already been swooning, she would have then, as he went up the stairs to the guestroom she was using and kicked the door shut after them. But not even then did he let her go. He crossed to the bed, leaned over and deposited her slowly on the mattress.

He straightened and Hayley's arms fell away. She stared up at him, mute, when he lifted one foot and then the other, pulling off her tennis shoes. They dropped to the floor, two soft thuds in the room that was silent except for the sounds of their breath, the rasp of the zipper on her jeans as he pulled it down and the rustle when the jeans followed. He yanked his shirt off, and she pulled off hers and groaned when the collar got caught up in her ponytail holder. “I’m stuck,” she nearly wailed.

He laughed softly and knelt on the bed next to her. “Hold on. You’re going to make it worse.” He nudged her shoulder so she was on her side, her back toward him, and she felt his fingers against the back of her head for a moment.

Then the stretchy collar was loose, her hair was falling free and he slid the shirt over her head. “All better,” he murmured and she felt his lips on her shoulder. Then the center of her back.

She fell weakly forward onto her stomach when he nudged, and shivered when his fingers slowly trailed down her spine, hooked in the edge of her plain cotton panties, and pulled them, too, down her legs. And this time, when the mattress dipped again under his weight and she felt the singeing heat of his skin against hers, there was only skin.

His arms surrounded her and she turned until they were flush and her breath hissed out of her. Everything about him was hard.

Except his eyes.

She could get lost forever in his eyes.

"I should have showered," he murmured.

"Later." Impatience suddenly ruled and she slid her thighs along his and took him in with an arch of her back.

He let out a low, choked oath.

Breathing fast, shuddering against the indescribable sense of fullness, she stared up at him through her lashes. "Is there a problem?"

"You tell me." In less than a breath, he'd anchored her wrists in one hand above her head and tilted her hips with his other, sinking even more deeply.

She gasped, pleasure unlike anything she'd

ever known rocketing through her. “No,” she managed faintly. “No…oh, *Seth*…no problem.”

His teeth flashed. And then he began moving, and words ceased to exist and all she could do was feel as he drove them both straight into oblivion.

Chapter Eight

It was the sound of Moose whining and gnawing on the other side of the door that finally roused them sometime later.

Seth untangled his legs from hers, pushed off the bed and turned on the lamp sitting on the nightstand.

With unabashed pleasure, Hayley watched his considerable naked glory as he crossed the room and opened the door.

"Moose, stop," he said.

Moose's whines immediately ceased. He

dropped his butt and his tail pounded the floor happily.

Hayley propped her head on her hand. Outside the bedroom window, the sky was dark. "I should probably let him out. He's not entirely accident proof yet when it comes to piddling in the house."

Seth scooped up his running shorts and pulled them on. The lazy gaze he ran over her made her hot. "I'll do it."

It was only after she could hear him and the dog going down the stairs that she realized she'd been so busy staring at his ridged abs that she hadn't offered a single objection.

She flopped onto her back and pressed her palm flat against her belly. Every muscle she possessed felt liquefied and the notion of lying there, feeling just as she did, for the rest of eternity, seemed extremely appealing. She closed her eyes, drifting on that lovely fantasy until she heard Moose's toenails scrabbling on the wood floor again.

A moment later, he raced through the door, launched himself into the air midway across the room and landed on the bed with a slathering woof.

Hayley turned her face away from the dog kisses, but he wasn't deterred, simply transferring his adoration to her arm and hands. "Good grief, Moose."

She finally left the bed to him and pulled on her short robe as she headed downstairs. "I think we're both in need of a shower now," she called as she reached the base of the stairs and turned toward the kitchen. "Which makes me think of at least one very interesting scenari—" She stopped abruptly at the sight that greeted her. "*—Oh*."

Seth was squared off on one side of the island against Tristan on the other. A third, hard-looking older man she didn't recognize was handling the old violin that Casey kept on a shelf.

Hayley tightened the sash of her robe. "Hello, Tristan." She gave Seth a quick look. Aside from his hands clenched at his sides, his expression was unreadable. "I didn't know you were here," she finished as if it were perfectly normal that he was even though it wasn't.

Tristan didn't look pleased. "Dr. Hayley Templeton." He pointed toward the stranger. "Coleman Black. The head of Hollins-Winword."

Dismay clutched inside her. She didn't know anything about Coleman Black but couldn't imagine any positive reasons for his presence. But she wasn't going to act as if she and Seth had been caught breaking some law, either, just because the situation was…delicate.

"Mr. Black," she greeted the stranger with a faint nod. "May I offer you gentlemen something to drink?"

At that, Seth moved away from the island.

"Nice try, Doc, but I don't think a show of good manners is gonna help things." He stopped when he reached her only long enough to squeeze her shoulder and brush his lips over her temple. "McGregor's more dangerous than you think. Be careful," he murmured before leaving the room.

She swallowed the plea for him to stay that she instinctively knew would prove pointless.

She wasn't a teenager caught making out in her parents' basement. She was a grown woman entitled to a life of her own and was going to act like it if it killed her. So she kept her focus on Tristan and his companion and raised her eyebrows slightly.

"When Cole stopped off here in Weaver to see Jason's status for himself, I thought it would be a good opportunity for him to meet you," Tristan explained in answer to her nonverbal query.

Hayley managed a smile she was miles away from feeling. "This is one of those times when a phone call in advance might have saved everyone some awkwardness." She lifted the violin out of Coleman Black's hands and placed it back on the shelf. The instrument had belonged to Casey's grandmother, and several months ago, Vivian had assisted in getting it repaired when it had been damaged.

Hayley didn't like seeing Coleman Black handle it.

And now he knew it.

She gestured toward the living room. "Have a seat," she suggested. "I'll just put on something more appropriate and be with you in a moment." She didn't wait for a response but sailed out of the kitchen.

As soon as she was out of sight, she tore up the stairs to the guest room, nearly tripping over her own feet in her haste.

Moose was snoring in the middle of the bed, his head lying on top of her tennis shoe. Seth's clothes were gone from the floor. She didn't make the mistake of thinking he had just gone to take that shower.

He had just gone, period.

She couldn't let herself think about the possible meanings behind that. Not yet. Not when she still had two other men downstairs to be dealt with first.

She pulled on her jeans and a sweater, twisted her hair back into a knot, stuffed her feet into leather loafers and went back down to do just that.

Rather than availing themselves of Casey and Jane's highly comfortable couch or chairs, the two men were sitting at the dining room table. That worked as far as Hayley was concerned. It made her think about the conference room at her office where she often conducted group sessions and meetings.

With that in mind, she pulled out the chair at the head of the table. Then she sat down with her hands folded together on top of it. Just because they were in authority where Seth and Hollins-Winword were concerned didn't mean they were in charge of *her*. Taking the position of power at the table might not matter to them, but it mattered to her.

Keeping a pleasant expression on her face, she focused on the newcomer. "Are you in town for long, Mr. Black?"

His aging, sun-weathered face creased in the faintest of smiles. Possibly amusement. Possibly appreciation for her unsubtle tactic. "I'm never anywhere for long, Dr. Templeton."

She wasn't sure if that was a warning or a simple statement of fact and decided that it really didn't matter. "Then I won't waste time here. If you're expecting me to break my patient's confidentiality and report on anything Mr. McGregor has said during our sessions, you're going to be disappointed." She let her gaze take in Tristan. "As I've already informed Tristan, it's my professional opinion that Mr. McGregor is not feigning his memory loss. I am happy to continue working with him, but unless or until he divulges that he has committed a crime—" she eyed them steadily "—which he hasn't even been charged with, or I believe he intends to bring harm to himself or others, my responsibility is to my patient. Ethically, I am bound to respect his right of privacy. With *everyone*," she added pointedly. "Not just you, but those in my…personal life."

"Your stance is commendable, Dr. Templeton." Coleman's voice was low. Gravelly. As if he smoked a lot, and perhaps that was his coping method given the responsibility of the position he held. "But there are other factors at work of which you may not be aware."

"Does it involve actual criminal charges being brought against my patient?" She caught the look that passed between the two men. "I'll take that as a no." She unfolded her hands, pressed her palms against the table and rose. "Then I believe we're done." She smiled calmly even though inside she was shaking. "I'll show you out."

And that's what she did.

She led the way to the front door, opened it and ushered them out onto the porch. "Safe travels, Mr. Black. Tristan, I'm sure we'll be talking again soon." She turned on her heel, went inside and closed the door on them.

And locked it.

Only then did she lean back against the wood panel and shudder.

"She just dismissed us," Cole murmured when he and Tristan found themselves standing on the porch in the chilly evening. He pulled a cigar out of his lapel pocket, stuck it between his teeth and started patting his other pockets for a light as they walked away from the house. "When's the last time you remember that happening?"

Tristan pursed his lips. He was pretty sure that, even back in the old days, such a thing had never occurred. Not with Cole, at any rate. "How much time have we got left before they yank Jason out of our hands?"

"A week." Cole seemed to give up on finding a match. "Maybe two, tops, if I pull in a few more favors." He tucked the cigar back in his pocket. "You didn't tell the good doctor that she had a time limit." It wasn't a question.

"I didn't think McGregor would hold out this long." Tristan exhaled a low oath. "He really can't remember. He was a good field agent. I don't want to believe he turned. And I don't want him to disappear into some black hole created by the Feds because one of *our* cases crept too close to one of theirs."

"It's a messy business," Cole agreed. They'd reached Tristan's SUV parked on the street. "What about this business with Banyon? He know how closely we're being watched on this one?"

"He will," Tristan said heavily. He didn't look

forward to the task of disciplining Seth when—unlike Cole—he'd always been a proponent of allowing their agents to actually *have* a personal life. But it was more than clear that Seth's self-control where the psychologist was concerned was nonexistent. Seth had admitted it himself when Tristan and Cole had shown up to see Hayley, only to catch the younger man looking *really* comfortable.

Tristan glanced back at the farmhouse owned by his nephew. Casey had been the analyst in charge of monitoring McGregor and his partners during their op and had taken their deaths hard. Even though he'd just married his perfect match and was happier than Tristan had ever seen him, his nephew was still struggling with his part in their undercover world. "You ever think that it's time we got out of the game?"

Cole snorted, his craggy face actually breaking out into a rare smile. He pulled open the passenger-side door. "Even after all these years, you're still green behind the ears if you actually think the game would ever let us."

Hayley eyed the door to Seth's apartment and blew out a breath. She'd tried calling him several times between her appointments that day, but he'd never answered. Nor had he made any attempt at returning the messages she'd left.

The last words he'd spoken to her had been about McGregor.

Now it was evening. And late because her Tuesday night group had gone longer than usual.

She chewed the inside of her cheek, balled up her knuckles and rapped on the apartment door. And when he didn't answer, she knocked harder.

"He's not there, honey," a voice said from nearby, and she looked down below Seth's apartment to see a skinny woman with fluorescent yellow hair watering her planters. "Saw him leave last night, bags and all."

Hayley's mouth dried. She clutched the

wrought-iron railing. “Are you Mrs. Carson?” She remembered him once mentioning his observant neighbor.

“I am.” The woman’s head bobbed, weirdly reminiscent of a pecking chicken. “Three of ’em,” she continued. “Suitcases, that is.” She peered up at Hayley. “You was here before.”

Hayley smiled weakly. “Several months ago.”

“Eh.” The woman waved her hand, dismissing that. “Only one I ever saw him bring here. Makes ya’ easy to remember. He didn’t tell ya’ he was leavin’?” Thankfully, she didn’t wait for an answer. “Same way George left me.” Her lip curled and she dumped the rest of the water in her watering can on her plants. “Never figured Seth for the type, but men are men, I always say.” She looked up again and wrinkled her nose. “Three suitcases is a lot of clothes. Don’t waste your time waitin’ on him to come back. That’s my advice.” Her head bobbed a few more times before she disappeared through her front door.

Hayley was still standing there, feeling numb, when she saw the curtains in Mrs. Carson's front window twitch.

She looked away and carefully made her way down the steps and back to her car, parked on the street in front of the small apartment building.

Don't trust me.

Seth's words circled inside her head. For all of his talk about relationships, he'd still told her that.

Twice.

Don't trust me.

She'd believed he was referring to McGregor. That Seth was warning her not to accidentally divulge anything about her patient that would jeopardize a possible case against Jason.

But maybe Seth had meant something different.

Her eyes burned as she climbed into her car.

Something very, very different.

Aching inside, she slowly put the car in motion, only remembering that she was supposed to be house sitting for Jane and Casey when she found herself parked in her own driveway and not theirs.

She shook her head sharply, scrubbed her palms down her cheeks and got out. She was here. She might as well say hello to her grandmother.

But when she let herself into the house, there was no sign of Vivian, either.

Oh, her clothes were definitely still there. Hayley was so upset that she checked. Vivian, for all of her idiosyncrasies, hadn't just *left* as it appeared Seth had.

"Is there a problem?" Her voice sounded thin in the silent house. Her lips twisted.

Yeah. There was a problem, all right.

She just didn't know how to recognize a one-night stand when it was staring her in the face. She was guilty of the same mistake so many others had made before her. Creating forever-afters out of molehills.

Shoving her hand through her hair, she left a note for Vivian that she'd dropped by and returned to Casey and Jane's place. Moving like an automaton, she clipped Moose to his lead and took him for a walk around the block. She did what she advised so many others to do.

She did the normal thing. The mundane and usual.

Because that's what it took, sometimes, to get through a breaking heart.

Her dad was mowing the lawn.

For as long as Hayley could remember, when the weather was good, that's what Carter Templeton did on a Saturday morning. Mowed the lawn.

And as strained as their relationship had been

since Vivian's arrival, that one simple act reminded Hayley that some things, at least, remained steady and true.

She didn't bother pushing the image of Seth out of her mind. By trying so hard not to think about him, all she'd succeeded in doing for the past week had been imagining him around every corner, just out of her sight. Hovering like some ghost. So she'd stopped trying. And she was still hoping her common sense would put those flights of fancy to rest, once and for all.

She picked up one of the two boxes sitting beside her that were still wrapped gaily in red and green Christmas paper and got out of the car she'd parked at the curb in front of her parents' house. She headed across the grass and stopped in the middle of an unmowed patch where Carter would be forced to stop and acknowledge her if he wanted to finish his routine.

She knew he wouldn't leave the job unfinished. That wasn't her father's way. And after another five minutes or so of standing in the surprisingly warm April sunshine with the spring-sweet smell of fresh grass clippings making her want to sneeze, he finally stopped pushing the mower, letting the motor die.

At fifty-eight, Carter Templeton was still a good-looking man. His dark hair was liberally shot with gray, but it sprang back from his square forehead as thick as ever. Even though his time in the army was more than thirty years past, his tall, spare body still possessed a military bearing. The familiar posture cheered her as much as his habitual weekly mowing.

"Hi, Daddy," she greeted.

His eyes were dark brown like hers and they narrowed as he took his time studying her. "You look like hell," he finally said.

Deflated, she pressed Vivian's Christmas album to her chest. "Well, gee, Dad. Thanks ever so much."

His lips thinned. "You have circles under your

eyes. It's your grandmother's doing. I warned you about her, but you wouldn't listen."

"The circles aren't because of Vivian," she replied. "They have nothing whatsoever to do with her." Because she'd come to Braden determined to make one part of her life feel less of a failure, she stepped around the lawn mower and reached up to kiss his cheek. "I love you, Dad. Just want to get that in there in case you make me forget later."

His brows lowered. "I love you, too," he returned gruffly. "That's why I can't understand what you're doing with *her*. Skunks don't change their stripes, missy."

"Vivian's not a skunk." A dirty pickup truck noisily chugged down the street and Hayley absently watched it turn the corner. "Finish the lawn," she suggested. "I'm going inside to say hello to Mom."

"Early for Christmas presents, isn't it?"

She patted the box. "Not early. Late. Four

months late." She headed for the house. "I'll see you inside when you're done."

She didn't wait for an answer. Just went through the front door and found her mother in the kitchen, where she was stirring the contents of a big pot at the stove. The radio was on and Meredith's bare feet were moving in time to the music. She was six years younger than Carter and as bohemian as he was conventional. Her glossy black hair streamed down her narrow back in ringlets and the bracelet around one of her ankles tinkled with the sound of small bells.

"What concoction are you boiling up now?"

Meredith whirled, her wildly colorful skirt flaring around her calves. "Hayley!" She left the long-handled spoon sticking out of the big pot and wrapped her arms around her, squeezing her hard. "I *told* Carter that today was going to be a beautiful day, and here you are!" She pushed away, looking up at Hayley with bright blue eyes. "Don't you look like a ray of sunshine?"

Hayley grimaced and set the box on the table by the window. "Daddy told me I looked like hell."

"Oh." Meredith swished her hand in the air dismissively. "Ignore him. He needs more prunes in his diet."

It was the first time Hayley had felt like laughing all week. Ever since Mrs. Carson had told her about Seth and his three—*count 'em, three*—suitcases. "You're too good for him." She repeated the words that she'd grown up hearing her father say, time and time again. "How're the Trips?"

"Busy as usual." Meredith went back to stirring her pot. "Ali's riding with another new partner. Greer's on night court and Maddie's still on adult probation."

"Only you would have a cop, a public defender and a social worker for daughters," Hayley said with a laugh. "I've been so busy I haven't had a chance to talk with them lately. And Rosalind?"

"Still working for her father's legal firm in Cheyenne." Meredith shrugged. "She really *is* too good for them."

Hayley squeezed Meredith's shoulders, knowing how hard her stepmother worked to maintain a relationship with her eldest daughter. "Any of them dating? Or is that still Arch's domain?" Last she'd checked, her older brother had a revolving door when it came to the opposite sex.

"Greer's been seeing someone for a few weeks. Haven't met him yet. What about you? Anyone special?"

Seth's ever-present image swam inside her head. "I thought there was." She went quiet for a moment. "Really special."

Meredith tsked. "I'm sorry, honey."

"So am I." Truer words she'd never spoken. Then she frowned as she looked into the unappealing, smelly muck inside the pot. "What is that?"

"Soap."

"Her latest hobby," Carter said, coming into the kitchen. He grabbed a coffee mug and filled it to the brim before pulling out one of the chairs and sitting at the table. "Smells like doody, if you ask me."

Hayley's smile felt wooden. Was "doody" the word former military men reserved for use around the women in their lives?

Of course, as she'd just indicated with Meredith, Hayley wasn't *in* Seth's life.

"It's lavender and olive oil." Meredith set an apple on the table next to Carter's coffee.

"Still stinks." But he gave her a fond pat on the rump as she danced her way back to the stove.

Hayley pulled out another chair and sat across from her dad. She pushed the gift toward him. "It's for you. I have another one in my car for Uncle David."

Carter immediately shook his head. "Then it's from the Queen of the Damned. No, thank you."

"Don't call your mother that," Meredith chided. "She gave birth to you."

"It's a wonder she didn't eat her young."

"Come on, Dad. Vivian Archer Templeton. You named Arch after her!"

"I named your brother after *her* father." He pushed the box away. "It's just a family name and your mother liked it."

His reaction wasn't any different than what Hayley had expected. She knew, of course, that the box contained the photo album that Vivian had put together herself. But she'd never had an opportunity to see the contents. So she started unwrapping it herself. "If you're not going to open it, I will."

Carter just shook his head and drank his coffee.

Meredith sat down in the chair next to Hayley

and watched curiously when she uncovered the fine, leather book and flipped it open.

"Oh, look." Meredith immediately pointed at the first baby picture. "Carter, you look just the same as you did as a baby! So precious."

He grunted softly. "Last I checked the mirror, I wasn't bald and toothless. Yet."

Meredith smiled and reached across the table to squeeze his hand. "You."

From the corner of her eye, Hayley saw her dad's hand turn beneath his wife's and squeeze back. "You," he replied softly.

A bittersweet lump lodged in Hayley's chest at the sight of the familiar exchange, but she kept glancing through the album. The Templeton sons had all been dark haired and good-looking. The earlier days were captured in black and white photos. Eventually colored Polaroids showed them in ski gear and swimwear. On golf courses and tennis courts. There weren't as many smiles on their faces as children ought to have, but it was clear from the chronicling that they'd all been athletic.

"No baseball or football?" She looked up at her dad.

He made a face. "Templetons didn't play sports like that." His voice turned mocking. "We had private schools and personal tutors and weekends at the club."

"This is Thatcher?" She held up the book to show one picture in particular of a well-built young man, arm hanging out of a convertible.

Carter nodded. Despite his rejection of Vivian's gift, he took the album from Hayley and studied the small picture more closely. "That Jag was his high school graduation gift." He closed the album with finality. "He went to a party after he got his diploma and he kept on driving. Was two years before David and I heard from him again. He warned us to get out while we could."

"Vivian told me what Thatcher believed about your father's death. And that he was wrong."

"Why would she admit now to making my father's life such a misery he drove off a cliff?"

"There's no proof he did it intentionally."

"There is no proof that he didn't." Hayley's father gave her a stern look. "Do you think I didn't look into it myself? That David didn't? The only one who knows the truth is my father. He died before I got to know him. But I know my mother all too well. She's self-involved, the worst possible snob and manipulative as hell." He lifted the edge of the album and let it fall heavily back to the table. "And she's got you doing her dirty work."

"She doesn't know I brought the albums. And I'm sorry that she was not a good mother to you, Dad. But she's never done anything to me and I'm tired of you making this an either-or situation. You're my father. I wouldn't be who I am today if not for you, and I love you."

He frowned. "And you're going to say you love *her*? You didn't know she existed until a few months ago."

"Actually, yes." Hayley realized it was true. "I've become very fond of Vivian. That doesn't make me love you less." She stood. "What makes the respect I've always had for you a little tarnished is your continued lack of compassion for a woman who has only wanted to tell you she's sorry for her mistakes. As if you've never made any of your own." She sent Meredith an apologetic look, left the album on the table and headed for the door. "I'm dropping off Uncle David's album at his place in case you feel the need to call and give him a warning."

Meredith hurried after her. "Honey, please. Stay."

Hayley gave her stepmother a hug. "I actually really can't. I've got things waiting for me in Weaver." She'd left Moose in Casey and Jane's backyard and hoped she wouldn't return to a dozen complaints from the neighbors that he'd barked the entire time. She'd have brought him with her if Meredith weren't allergic to pet dander. "All I wanted to do was bring the albums and see if I could get through to him."

"He'll come around," Meredith said for about the hundredth time over the past half a year. She squeezed Hayley's arm, accompanying her outside. "I miss seeing you."

"I miss seeing you, too. But the road between Weaver and Braden isn't one way. You can always come and visit me, as well." Her parents used to do so fairly often until Vivian's arrival. "Don't worry, though. I'll be sure to be in touch more often." Vivian couldn't be the only one who was ready to move forward in the face of disappointment.

Hayley would, as well.

At least when it came to her relationship with her family.

When it came to Seth's leaving?

She didn't need her PhD to know that getting over that was going to take a lot more time.

Chapter Nine

"I want to take him outside."

Tristan Clay's eyebrows rose over Hayley's abrupt demand. He tossed down his pen on the wide desk in his Cee-Vid office and gestured at the two chairs situated on the other side. "Good afternoon, Hayley. Come on in." His voice was dry.

She entered the office and closed the glass door behind her. From his vantage point, he could look out over the open floor plan of his gaming company. On that Monday afternoon, every desk was occupied and she couldn't help but think of all those workers in relation to the construction going on around town.

Weaver had started out as a ranching community. But Cee-Vid's booming success was certainly doing a good job of widening the gene pool.

"I'm sorry." She sat in the closest chair. "I should have called to tell you I was coming." She couldn't help the dark irony, nor—judging by his expression—was it lost on the man sitting across from her.

"Have you heard from him?"

Her hands tightened in her lap. She didn't make the mistake of thinking he meant McGregor. Nor did she want to talk about Seth. Not with this man and not with anyone else. "No. Ja—" She broke off, cognizant of their Cee-Vid surroundings. "My *patient*," she amended, "needs some fresh air. A change of scenery."

"Is this your idea or his?"

"Mine." Since she'd provided Jason with a stack of books, he hadn't asked for one other thing. He hadn't offered anything of significance, either. Nor had he consented to trying hypnosis. Which left her no further along in his care than they'd been a week ago. "Even convicted criminals are allowed a little time in the sun."

Tristan sat forward, folding his big hands on top of the desk. He was an exceptionally tall man—more Paul Bunyan, she'd always thought, than James Bond.

"That presents a security challenge," he said.

She shrugged. "I'm sure you have more than adequate means to handle any challenge."

His lips twitched. "You impressed the hell out of Coleman Black."

"I wish I could say the same about him." She didn't smile. "The more I learn about your—" she waved her hand expressively "—whatever, the less impressed I become. Unless your armed friends down in the basement decide to stop me, I intend to take my patient up to the land of the living for a breath of fresh spring air."

"And by doing so, you could be putting yourself and others in danger."

"If Ja—" She broke off again, pressing her lips together. "He has had ample opportunity to try and hurt me and he has not."

"You might want to be more careful where you put your trust."

The words felt like a blow to her midsection, but Tristan didn't need to know that. "I didn't say I trusted him. Only that it is my considered opinion he is unlikely to show violence toward me."

"Sounds like the long way of saying you trust him," Tristan said dryly. He sat back in his chair and watched her through hooded eyes. "I'll make arrangements for tomorrow afternoon," he finally said.

Satisfied that she'd gotten what she'd come

for, she nodded and stood. "Thank you." She reached for the door and pulled it open.

"If it helps any, I know he didn't want to leave." Tristan's words followed her and her shoulders went stiff. Once again, he wasn't referring to McGregor.

Though she didn't intend to respond, she found herself looking back at the man. "It's not the leaving. It's the way he did it." Then, feeling as if she'd just reopened a barely healing vein, she left.

She met McGregor at Willow Park. They arrived in separate vehicles: she in her conservative little sedan, Jason in a black SUV driven by two Hollins-Winword guards.

From Seth's rooftop vantage point among the houses under construction across the street, he watched Hayley and McGregor through the scope on his rifle. There were no construction workers on site today, and he knew Tristan had arranged that. Seth also knew the man had a security team spread out all through the park. Thanks to Adam's heads-up about McGregor's field trip, Seth had already been in place long before they took up their positions.

He knew where they were.

They just didn't know about *him*.

It had been five years since he'd been a sniper with the US Army. But even though his analytical abilities were what made him valuable to Hollins-Winword, he'd maintained his rifle proficiency the same way he'd maintained his physical fitness. There were some things that a ranger never left behind no matter how many years passed.

If it meant perching in the rafters of a house still in the framing stage for ten hours just to see for himself that Hayley was protected during the thirty minutes she was being allowed outside with McGregor, then he'd do it every day of the week and twice on Sundays.

Tristan might have thought he'd effectively banished Seth from the area, but Seth had had other ideas. He'd undoubtedly burned his bridges with the man by going AWOL instead of reporting in at the agency's Denver office as instructed, but Seth was beyond caring. After he'd left his apartment, he'd bought a bus ticket in Braden bound for Denver, stashed his nonessential gear in the lockers at the station there and hitched a ride from a trucker back to Weaver.

He knew how to disappear when he needed to.

But he didn't know how to stop himself from watching over Hayley any more than he knew how to stop himself from caring.

Because somewhere between watching her sneak out of his apartment on a predawn January morning and unraveling a leash from her legs on a cool April evening, he'd realized he cared a helluva lot more about her than he had ever cared about seeing McGregor face charges for Manny and Jon's deaths.

He shifted his hand slightly, following her and McGregor's progress along the sidewalk. She walked at a leisurely pace but he saw how she hesitated almost imperceptibly as they neared the playground equipment. He could see her lips moving. He knew she and McGregor were having a conversation even if he couldn't tell what it was about.

She was wearing a dark gray skirt and jacket and low shoes. Her long shining hair was pulled back to the middle of her head in its usual ponytail and it drifted around in the constant breeze. If she was upset about Seth's absence, there was nothing in her outward appearance that showed it.

His cross-hair settled gently on her companion. McGregor was even skinnier than the last time Seth had seen him. The jeans he wore hung on his frame; his face was pale and almost skeletal. And while Seth watched, McGregor turned his face toward the sky and closed his eyes, his lanky shoulders visibly rising and falling.

Seth's jaw tightened. He didn't want to feel sympathy for the man who had—more likely than not—betrayed his partners.

A movement on his periphery alerted him to the presence of a young couple entering the park from the other side. Tristan could arrange for construction workers to have a day off, but he couldn't control the actions of residents in the area without bringing more unwanted attention. The couple seemed oblivious to anything other than the baby stroller they were pushing. New parents, judging by their hovering, nervously excited body language.

Did Hayley ever think about becoming a mother?

Seth shifted slightly, getting his focus back where it belonged.

McGregor had pulled off the hospital-style

slippers he'd been wearing and was walking around in the grass. Even in the short two weeks since Seth had been there with Hayley, it had thickened and turned dark green. McGregor moved over to a tree and lined his spine up against it before bending his knees and slowly sitting down against it. Hayley joined him and tucked her legs together neatly to one side of her. Seth could see their lips moving as they talked and wished to hell he could hear what they were saying.

But all he could hear was the murmur of the couple's voices as they soothed the baby who'd started crying as they headed back out of the park.

His gaze centered again on Hayley's profile. She looked so calm. So peaceful. Her lips moved a lot less than McGregor's did. She was obviously listening more. Giving her patient the space to do the talking.

Seth's personal experience with therapists had been somewhat different.

But then, he'd been eighteen and every adult around him had been more interested in talking him out of his belief that his father's partner had engineered his dad's death than hearing why Seth believed so strongly that it had been so.

In the time since—until he'd met Hayley, anyway—he'd never had much use for therapists.

His practiced gaze periodically swept the area. He could see the Hollins-Winword detail monitoring the park's perimeter and slowly, inch by inch, some of the stress began draining from his body as nothing more disastrous occurred than Hayley absently swatting at a fly with a wave of her hand.

Nevertheless, it wasn't until a half hour later, when McGregor's two guards walked him back to the SUV and drove away, that Seth finally lay down his rifle with a hand that was strangely shaking.

He blew out a long breath and flexed his hands,

blaming the tremors on lack of practice even though he knew the truth was entirely different.

Maybe he needed a shrink, after all.

He rested his chin on his crossed arms and watched Hayley. She'd stood, too, when the guards had taken McGregor once more. But she didn't go immediately to her small car in the parking lot.

Instead, she moved over to the swings and sat in the same one Seth had pushed her on. But she didn't swing today. She just sat there motionless, her head lowered slightly while the faint breeze flirted with her long ponytail.

He very nearly lowered himself from the rafters to go to her. Found himself even starting to when a sheriff's cruiser trolled up the street and pulled to the curb. He could see Hayley's blond friend sitting behind the wheel as she hailed Hayley through the opened window. "Colbys tonight?" he heard her say.

Hayley left the swing, not answering until she reached the car, and when she did, her voice was too low for Seth to hear. Then the car drove off, and Hayley folded her arms over her chest, seeming to study the buildings across from her.

Seth waited, motionless; it felt as if she looked straight through his hiding place.

There was no way she'd be able to see him, though. For the past week he'd been blending into the woodwork. When he hadn't been keeping an eye on her, he'd been watching the safe house.

A moment later, she returned to her car and drove away, too.

Silently, Seth unloaded the rifle, broke it down and left the construction site.

It was a long while, though, before his hands stopped shaking. But his unease wasn't ever going to go away. Not until he knew that Hayley was finished for good with McGregor.

A strange man was in her kitchen.

Hayley stopped short at the sight of the bald man staring into her open cabinets before she remembered. "You must be Mr. Montrose." She set down the bags of groceries on her kitchen table and stuck out her hand. "My grandmother said you were coming. I'm Hayley."

The man gave her hand a brief, limp shake. He wiped his hand on his white apron that, she had a strong suspicion, was actually starched. "It's not *Mr.* Montrose." He had a faintly British accent. "It's only Montrose."

"Okay, uh, Montrose." She tried very hard not to stare, but he was wearing a black suit beneath the apron, along with a blinding white shirt and an honest-to-God bowtie. She gestured at the grocery bags. "I've been out stocking up."

"Mmm." He didn't look impressed. "Mrs. Templeton didn't adequately prepare me for the conditions here."

"Well." Hayley spread her arms, taking in her small kitchen. "It has always worked for me."

His expression told her what he thought about that.

"Speaking of my grandmother—" she tried a

tentative smile that he did not return "—do you know where she is?"

"Mrs. Templeton had an appointment with her attorney." He peered into one of the bags, pulling the paper aside with a bony finger. "Dear Lord," he said under his breath.

Hayley's smile became forced. Vivian had called him a prima donna, and so far, he was exhibiting the signs. "When did you arrive?"

"Last evening." He pulled a head of lettuce from the bag with the same expression she probably wore doing doody duty. "This little village of yours doesn't even possess a proper airport."

"And yet, we manage to survive," she couldn't help saying. "How long did you work for my grandmother?"

"Twenty years."

Not long enough for him to have been with Vivian when her father was still living at home. But if Montrose was a taste of the snootiness that Carter claimed had been pervasive in the

Templeton home, at that moment she wasn't all that sure she blamed him for wanting to get away from it.

"That's a long time," she said. "I am sure she's pleased you're here." Because he seemed so disturbed by the contents of her grocery bags, Hayley began unloading them herself. Mostly fruit and vegetables that she put away in the refrigerator, along with the head of lettuce that had seemed just fine to her when she'd purchased it on her way home from the uneventful outing with her patient in Willow Park.

"Of course she is pleased that I am here," Montrose said, looking offended that there could *possibly* be another point of view. "Who wouldn't be? I am Montrose."

"Yes." She tucked the bags away in a cupboard and edged toward the door. "You are indeed. I'll just, um, leave you to it, then." She backed out of the kitchen, never more anxious to leave her own home.

As soon as she escaped, though, a silver car bumped over the curb and jerked to a stop.

She wasn't sure which was more out of place: the car itself, or the fact that Vivian climbed out from behind the wheel of it.

Feeling more than a little bemused, Hayley approached the large sedan with the very distinctive hood ornament. "Vivian," she greeted. "Is that a—"

"A Rolls, dear." Vivian tugged the cropped hem of her jacket around her narrow hips and stepped up onto the curb, not seeming the least bothered by the fact that she'd parked the Rolls-Royce's front tire up on that curb, too. "It's *used* of course, though the official term is pre-owned, I believe. As if that makes it more desirable. But it was the only thing I could get on short notice."

"Is there even a dealership in the state?"

Vivian dismissed the question with a wave of her hand. "I leave those details to Stewart."

She reached Hayley and tucked her arm through hers. "Stewart St. James," she added. "My attorney."

"There's an attorney here named Stewart St. James?"

"Don't be dense, dear. He's in Pittsburgh, naturally. He's handled my affairs since the dawn of time."

"I thought, um, Montrose told me you were at an appointment with your attorney."

"An attorney." Vivian made a face. "I would hardly call Tom Hook *my* attorney. I had to meet him in a barn. I feel certain he had cow dung on his boots."

"Then why were you meeting with him?" Hayley pushed open the front door again for Vivian to enter the house.

"To sign my new will. Stewart sent Mr. Hook all of the details." Vivian sailed into the kitchen. "Montrose, dear. Are you making yourself comfortable?"

Hayley winced at the response Vivian received to that. But Vivian just laughed as if she were used to him. And, Hayley supposed, after employing the man for twenty years, she probably was.

Nevertheless, Hayley chose not to follow Vivian into the kitchen. One brief dose of the chef was enough to last her for a while. She flipped disinterestedly through her mail until Vivian returned bearing one of Hayley's fat coffee mugs that seemed even fatter with Vivian holding it as if it were a fine china cup.

"Sit," Vivian bid, waving at the couch and chairs. "I'm glad you're here. I have a lot of news."

Hayley sank down on her usual chair. "A chef and a Rolls-Royce aren't enough?"

"The Phantom is nothing." Vivian dismissed the car as if it had come out of a Cracker Jack box. She sat on the couch and set down the mug. "About my will. Stewart, of course, will act as executor and he will continue to advise you when—"

"Whoa." Hayley waved her hands. "Hold on. What do *I* have to do with your will?"

"I told you I would be leaving everything to you. Lock, stock and barrel, as Mr. Hook put it." Vivian peered at her. "Are you certain you're not under some effect from your young man leaving town?"

Hayley was certain that she *was* but she had no desire to discuss with her grandmother the fact that she kept imagining Seth was nearby, even though she had proof otherwise. Vivian would likely tell her that she was as crazy as she was beginning to feel.

"I remember you saying that, Vivian, but I didn't think you were serious."

"I would hardly joke about the matter," Vivian assured her dryly. "At last estimate, my estate was well over seventy—"

"—I don't want to know!" Feeling alarmed, Hayley pushed to her feet.

"For a psychologist, you're doing a good job of acting like an ostrich," Vivian pointed out. "But fine. If you don't want to know yet what you'll be worth, that's your decision." She shook her head as if the idea was unfathomable. "You'll know soon enough."

"Don't even talk that way, Vivian. You're going to be around for a long time." She looked out the window at the carelessly parked luxury car. "Just, um, don't drive any more than you have to, okay?"

"I haven't enjoyed driving for years. I've been trying to find a driver, but so far, the few people I've spoken with have been entirely unsuitable."

A chef. A driver. And Hayley also couldn't forget the housekeeper that Vivian had mentioned wanting. Along with a "suitable" house.

"How are you advertising for this driver?"

"Mr. Bumble has been referring people to me."

Bubba. The cook at Ruby's was referring applicants to her grandmother.

"This is all quite…interesting," Hayley said. "I'm a little concerned that you're making a lot of plans so quickly. Are you that certain you want to go to such expense just to stay in Weaver when you already have everything you're used to back in Pittsburgh?"

"Will you come home to Pittsburgh with me?" Vivian smiled slightly, obviously getting her answer from Hayley's slack-jawed expression. "I thought not. You, like your father and all of the Templeton men before him, clearly have some fascination with the *Wild West*." She emphasized the phrase with a good dollop of disdain. "It's unfathomable to me, but there's no accounting for taste." She stood, smoothing the back of her short hair. "This is very simple, dear. I don't care about Wyoming. I care to have my granddaughter near me. I will make things suitable here so that I may be near *you*."

She couldn't help but be touched, regardless of Vivian's snootiness. It wasn't up to Hayley to say how or where her grandmother should use her money. So she rose and gave her a quick hug. "Give some thought to keeping the Rolls," she suggested. "I'm not sure how well it will perform come wintertime when there are a few feet of snow on the ground and the plow hasn't made it through yet."

"Perhaps." Vivian tapped her lips, looking thoughtful. "We can discuss it over dinner." She gave Hayley a droll look.

She snuck a look toward the kitchen doorway, beyond which she could hear Montrose's occasional exclamations.

Not joyful ones, either.

"What sort of dinner did you have in mind?"

As if on cue, Montrose stormed into the living room. "I *cannot* cook in this kitchen. It is an atrocity."

Hayley grimaced, wondering how much poor

taste she'd be showing if she offered up the use of Casey and Jane's gourmet kitchen. Jane had nearly bent over backward ensuring that Hayley felt at home there. But that was because she was a dear friend. And Jane had been desperate to find someone to watch their wayward puppy because everyone else in Casey's family had refused.

"I've already made plans to meet Sam at Colbys," she said. "Come with us."

Montrose huffed and fled back to the kitchen, obviously offended.

Hayley lowered her voice to a whisper. "Vivian, are you sure you wouldn't rather just hire Bubba on a permanent basis?"

Vivian laughed merrily. If anything, it seemed to Hayley that the more outrageous Montrose sounded, the happier her grandmother was. "In my day an attractive young woman didn't voluntarily go around using a man's name. But I suppose Colbys will do."

Vivian's capitulation was almost stunning. "Okay," Hayley said, trying to cover her surprise. "I need to check in at my office for an hour or so. You won't change your mind before I come back to get you?"

Vivian waved her hand. "I have a car now, remember? There's no need to come back to get me when I can meet you there."

Hayley eyed her grandmother. At least one person in Hayley's family seemed to be making positive progress. "All right, then. We'll meet at Colbys."

Chapter Ten

"Who's the old lady?"

Hayley eyed Jason. She'd just spent the past two hours attempting hypnosis with him—and failing as miserably as he'd warned her she would. "I beg your pardon?"

"The one with the expensive car when you and your cop friend went out last night."

She wasn't even aware that she'd slid her hand into her pocket until she felt the hard outline of the panic button. She couldn't carry the thing into the room without hearing Seth's parting words to her.

"The gorillas talking again?"

As usual, Jason sat on the bed with his back against the wall. It wasn't so he could look at her where she was standing. It was so he never had his sight away from the door, which was directly behind her. "They're always talking."

And she didn't want to be the subject of the guard's chatter. Yes, it was people's nature to talk. But it seemed to her that given their responsibilities, they could be a little more discreet around the man they were guarding. "She's my grandmother."

"Why are you playing around in the dungeon with me if you're rich?"

"I'm not rich." She didn't want to think about Vivian's intentions where her will was concerned. "And I'm not playing around." She might as well have been, considering how little she was helping Jason. Though Jason had seemed calmed by the park outing—talking about simple things like the books she'd delivered to him and his craving for lemon meringue pie—it hadn't been as productive as she'd hoped. The fresh air certainly hadn't helped him sleep any better than usual. And this afternoon, trying to guide him back to what should have been simple childhood memories had been an outright failure.

"Then why are you here? Why keep coming? The money they pay you that good?"

She resisted the urge to look at her watch and sat back down in her chair. "What are you hoping to hear, Jason? That I'm here for the paycheck? That I'm inherently nosy and like poking a stick at people's minds and emotions? Or that I'm here because I believe in you?"

He looked away and she sighed, knowing she'd hit on the truth. "I believe you experienced something so deeply traumatic in Central America that your mind isn't ready yet to let those memories back in. I can't tell you that

I believe you're innocent, Jason. But I *also* can't tell you I believe you were responsible for your colleagues' deaths. My purpose here is to help you regain the memories. Not only of what happened then, but of the rest of your life, as well. The sister who is only a name to you. The woman you married. The parents who raised you. You had a life. When the need to let all of that back in surpasses the need to suppress it, you'll remember."

"Who is Banyon?"

She felt herself pale and wanted to curse because, of course, her patient noticed. "What have you heard about him?"

"He's AWOL."

She started. "What?"

"Didn't know that, did you?" He waited a beat. "He was supposed to go to Denver. Never showed."

Her mouth felt dry. "And that's of interest to you because…?"

"Because he's of interest to you." Jason swung his legs off the bed so abruptly that she was startled. But all he did was sit forward, his hands clenched between his thighs. "Don't worry," he muttered. "I'm not the proverbial freaking patient falling for his doctor. But you're the only friend I've got."

"I'm not your friend. Nor am I your enemy." And despite all of her best efforts, there was something about the troubled man that tugged at her sympathy. She stood and pulled her hand from her pocket—and the button. "You have more people trying to help you than you know, Jason." Tristan Clay and Coleman Black being the most important. As for Seth…she wasn't going to be foolish enough to assume anything about him.

She tapped her knuckles on the door. "I'll be back tomorrow."

"They're saying he's AWOL because of you."

She didn't react. But she did vow then and

there to suggest to Tristan that he remind his guards to mind their tongues.

"Watch out for him."

Hayley wished the guard would hurry up and open the door. She knocked on it again. "He said the same about you." The door finally opened.

"Then maybe he's smarter than both of us." Jason's dark voice followed her as she left.

She didn't wait to hear the heavy door shut again as she went into the observation room. "I want to see the log," she told Adam, who was manning the room.

He looked surprised but immediately handed the book to her. She flipped back through the pages. Seth's name was there several times; his scrawl seemed to scream impatience on the white sheets. His sign-ins stopped, though, a week ago. She traced her finger over the last of his entries. The rest of the lines were filled, more or less neatly, with the comings and goings of the guards and, less often, Tristan Clay.

"Bring your guest a steak from Colbys for dinner tonight," she told Adam. "And lemon meringue for dessert." She retrieved her briefcase and left, not particularly caring what the guard would make of her uncharacteristic orders.

She returned to her office and wrote up her notes on her session with Jason, held her usual weeknight support group and finally locked up the office for the day and headed to Casey and Jane's.

She let herself in through the front door. Moose didn't greet her as he usually did, and alarm raced through her. Torn between calling for him—just to prove she was being nervous over nothing when he would come bounding toward her with his ears and tongue flopping—and retreating to her car, all she could do was stand there in the dark foyer, frozen.

"It's all right, Doc." The deep, soft voice came out of the shadows, and her knees went weak.

From out of the shadows, Seth took shape in front of her. "I didn't mean to scare you."

She fumbled with the light switches on the wall; finally finding the one that controlled the lamp on the entry table against the wall, she flipped it and sucked in another breath.

He was dressed in camouflage pants and shirt. But it was his expression that looked hellish. As if he hadn't slept a minute since he'd left her in this very house with Tristan and Coleman Black. "What are you doing here?" Her tone was abrupt. "How'd you get in?"

Where have you been?

Why did you leave?

She asked neither.

"You left the back door unlocked." He didn't smile. "You shouldn't do that."

She was fairly certain that a locked door wouldn't keep Seth from entering anywhere he wanted to go.

Or from exiting.

She carefully set her briefcase on the table. “Where’s Moose?”

“Out back. I ran him around the yard for a while to tire him out. He was pretty excited when I got here.”

The puppy wasn’t the only one. She swallowed. Her mouth felt unaccountably dry. “What are you doing here?” she asked again.

“You’re running out of time with Jason.”

“Of course,” she murmured. “Everything keeps coming back to Jason. That’s why you’re back as unexpectedly as you disappeared. Not… not because of me, but—”

Seth’s hands suddenly latched around her arms and he yanked her close, covering her mouth with his in a hard, fast kiss.

Just as abruptly, he set her away from him again. “Everything is about you,” he said flatly.

Her lips were stinging and her legs were shaking, but she forced herself to walk past him into the kitchen as if her world weren’t careening around in utter confusion. “You’re supposed to be in Denver. At least that’s what I’ve heard.” From her patient, which was a painful irony as far as she was concerned. “So why aren’t you?”

“Because if I’m in Denver, I can’t keep you safe.”

“You left,” she said flatly. “The only one I need to feel safe from is you.”

The shadows under his eyes seemed to get darker. “I didn’t leave.”

She gaped. “You don’t expect me to take that seriously, do you?”

“I’ve been in Weaver all along,” he said evenly. “I just needed to make sure it looked like I’d left. So nobody can later suggest your judgment about McGregor had been influenced.”

She shook her head. “You’re warning me about him. He’s warning me about you.” She ignored the way Seth’s jaw tightened even more at that. “What do you mean I’m running out of time?”

“Tristan’s…custody…of McGregor has an expiration date. The federal government wants him back, and they're getting impatient."

"Tristan hasn't told me that. You expect me to believe he told *you* when you're not supposed to be involved in any of this at all?"

"There are other sources than Tristan."

"Comforting," she said facetiously.

"This time next week, McGregor will be gone. So whatever magic tricks you've got in your bag, you'd better pull them out now."

"There's no magic. With time—" She broke off and turned away. She flipped on the outside light and spotted Moose sleeping in the bed of petunias. "Were you in the park yesterday?"

He waited a beat. "I was nearby."

Her stomach hollowed out a little. "I can't decide what's more disturbing. Thinking that I was imagining you there or knowing that I wasn't. Have you been following me all this time? Watching me?"

"I've been watching him." His voice was flat.

"Yes. I could see you in the park yesterday. I was prepared to take him out if he made a move against you."

She trembled. "What is that supposed to mean?"

"I was there with a sniper's rifle, Doc. And I don't miss."

The image that hurtled into her mind stole her breath. "Jason's not a danger to me," she whispered.

"I know you think that. But I'm still not willing to take that on faith. I'm not going to rest until he's gone from here once and for all."

"Then you should be glad my time with him is running out," she said huskily. "So why warn me at all?"

"Because you're his shrink. You deserve to know."

"So you'll tell me the truth, even though you're prepared to shoot him?"

"I'm prepared to do whatever it takes to keep

you safe. If I could stop you from ever getting within five feet of him, I would. But I know that's not going to happen. So, instead…I… watch." His voice went hoarse. "And hope to hell I don't miss if it comes down to that."

She shuddered wildly. "You're scaring me."

"Then that makes two of us." He stepped forward and gently wrapped his arms around her. He didn't try to tell her that everything was fine when it was so patently obvious that it wasn't. He just held her. Until her shaking stopped and her resistance ebbed and she simply leaned into him. Into this man whose basic need was to protect.

And then he drew her upstairs and into the guest bathroom. Wordlessly, he turned on the shower, letting the water heat up while he unzipped her skirt and pushed it to her feet, and then worked the buttons down the front of her blouse free and slid it from her shoulders. When he turned to check the water, she stepped out of her flats as well as the skirt around her feet and pulled her bedraggled ponytail loose. He stepped behind her and she felt his wet fingers undoing the hooks of her bra. He tugged her panties down and without looking at her, pulled back the clear shower glass door and urged her beneath the hot, soothing spray.

But when he went to close the shower door again she stopped him. "You, too."

His jaw canted slightly. "You need—"

"—you," she cut him off. "I need you." The admission flowed out of her as surely as the water flowed over her shoulders, with no hope of being shut off as easily. "You don't have to make love to me. I just don't want you to go."

In answer, he tugged his T-shirt over his head. Unlaced his combat boots and pulled them off. Then came his socks. Then the camouflage pants, which on him were part of his history and not some macho fashion choice. When his clothes were piled among hers, he stepped into the shower with her and closed the door.

"You looked like a soldier," she murmured.

"I was a soldier. Now I'm just a man." His arm brushed hers as he reached for her bottle of shampoo and moved around her until his broad back blunted most of the shower spray. "Turn around."

She turned, swiping her hand over her wet face, and went still when she felt his hands on her head.

He wasn't washing his own hair. He was washing hers.

She blinked hard against a sudden rush of tears. "You were young when you enlisted."

"Eighteen." His fingertips massaged her scalp.

He'd told her he'd served for fifteen years and been out for five. "So you're thirty-eight?"

"Yep."

He worked his way lower, around her occipital, and she let out a long breath of pleasure.

"After the past week," he murmured, "I feel a helluva lot older."

Her head fell back a little. "When you were a ranger did you—" She broke off, not sure she should even ask. "Travel a lot?" she finished instead.

His hands moved to her shoulders, and he switched spots with her to rinse the suds from her hair. Which also left them facing one another. "Ask what you really want to ask, Doc."

She stared up into his face. His eyelashes were spiked with water, making them seem even darker. "How do you know that's not what I was going to ask?"

His fingers finally slid away from her hair. "I traveled a lot." He reached for the bar of soap and began working up a lather, but his eyes stayed on hers. "And yesterday wasn't the first time I've been prepared to put a bullet in somebody. It wasn't the first time I didn't have to. Unfortunately, more often than not, I did have to."

"How did you cope?"

He slid his sudsy hands over her shoulders. Down her arms, up the insides of her elbows. "You're the shrink. How does a soldier cope when they've killed another?"

"You weren't just a soldier. You're a person. I want to know how *you* coped."

"By knowing I did what needed to be done to keep somebody else from dying. By completing the mission." He slid the bar of soap over her hips. Worked it down the outsides of her thighs. Her calves. Then he turned her again to face the water and worked his way up again.

When he reached the small of her back, his hands slowed. "Move your hair."

She pulled her wet hair in front of her shoulder and his soapy hands slid slowly up her back. Steam was rising around them, curling up the glass enclosure and sneaking out above the top.

Even though his touch was gentle, as carefully unprovocative as it could ever be, she still felt steam rising inside her.

"Didn't matter how many missions there were, though." His fingers slid over her waist, slowing as they glided upward beneath her arms, along her ribs and brushed the outer curves of her breasts. He stepped closer and his head dropped as he kissed the top of her shoulder. "Never got to rid the world of the man who got away with killing my old man when I was eighteen."

She inhaled, sliding her arms over his when they circled her waist, keeping her still when she would have turned to face him again. "What happened?"

"He was a partner in an outfitter company, and they were down in Corpus Christi to meet with a guy who wanted to buy them out." His voice was low, rumbling against her shoulder. "Dad didn't want to sell. Marcus, his partner, did. They'd been arguing about it for months.

Bad arguments. The two of 'em went out on a boat while they were down there. Only one came back."

She rubbed her palm over his arm, feeling the hard tendons beneath the water-slick hair and flesh. "I'm sorry." No wonder he was so adamant about Jason's guilt. It wasn't suspicion that ruled him. It was personal history. "What happened?"

"The DA wouldn't prosecute a case he considered unwinnable and Marcus walked, with a minor fortune in his pocket thanks to the store my pop loved. I tried to get a copy of the investigation. To see for myself. But the records were lost."

"What about your mother? Where was she?"

"She didn't want a kid. Especially one from a working-class guy like my old man. It was okay to mess around with somebody she considered low class, but beyond that?" He shook his head. "She dumped me with him when I was a baby and never looked back. It's surprising she bothered having me at all."

"Any other family?" But Hayley was afraid she already knew the answer.

"None that mattered."

Her chest squeezed. "Seth."

He ran the soap up between her breasts, stepping closer until there was no space left between her back and his front and she shivered despite the steaming water.

"Marcus was like a second father to me. But the second he could, he sold the business." His voice was short. "I enlisted. Never saw him again."

His empty hand covered her breast. "And that's the short history of Seth Banyon," he murmured and kissed the side of her neck. "Psychology one-oh-one, probably." His thumb roved her over tight nipple, sending heat straight to her core.

"You're not even close to a textbook." Her voice was faint and she let out a low moan when his other hand slid over her abdomen, gliding down between her thighs. “I said you didn’t have to…” Her voice trailed off as his long fingers replaced the soap that fell unheeded to the shower floor.

“There’s ‘have to,’” his voice deepened as his slick fingers moved, “and there’s ‘need to.’” The hard length of him prodded against her. “Of all people, you should understand the difference.”

She shuddered, melting around his fingers. “Take what you need,” she whispered, tilting her head back and pulling his mouth to hers.

And he did. He took, and took, until she convulsed around his long, clever fingers, and then he turned her around, lifted her shaking legs around his hips and took some more, pressing her back against the glossy tile wall until she cried out his name.

And then, he gave.

She almost didn’t hear the call when it came hours later. And even then, she might not have if it weren’t for Moose’s barking.

Seth was already sitting up in bed, his bare shoulders visible in the gleam of moonlight through the blinds. "I'll let him out."

She rolled out of bed. There was never any happy reason for her phone to ring in the middle of the night. Usually, it meant the sheriff was dealing with some official crisis that necessitated a counselor. "My cell phone is ringing, too. I left it downstairs." She nudged his hard shoulder. He'd admitted how little sleep he'd gotten over the past week. She was still shocked at the lengths he'd gone to. "Go back to sleep." She scooped up her robe from the chair and pulled it on as she hurried out of the room.

The ringing stopped before she made it down the stairs, though Moose's barking didn't. She let him out into the backyard and was just retrieving her phone from her briefcase pocket when Seth came down the stairs, too. "I told you to sleep," she said.

He gave her a look and finished zipping up his cargo pants.

She dragged her eyes away from his bare chest and focused on her phone.

Dread sank through her. Not the sheriff at all. "It was Tristan." She recognized the number. "He didn't leave a message."

"If it's about McGregor, he wouldn't."

"Who else would it be about but Jason?" She sat down on the bottom tread of the staircase and redialed the number.

Tristan picked up on the second ring. "Put Banyon on."

She winced and held out the phone to Seth. "He wants you."

Without expression, he took the phone and held it to his ear. "Yeah."

Hayley rubbed her hands up and down her arms, watching Seth's face. She couldn't hear what Tristan was saying, but considering the man knew Seth was with *her* when he wasn't supposed to be, she could imagine.

And a few moments later, without having spoken another word, the call was done. Seth held out the phone.

"Please don't tell me that he's fired you because of me."

"He turned in Jason to the sheriff two hours ago."

"What? You told me I had a week!"

When she didn't take the phone, he set it on the table next to her briefcase.

She grabbed the wooden banister and pulled herself to her feet. Not once had she heard Seth refer to her patient by his first name. "Turned him in to the *sheriff*," she said. Not the federal government. "You mean voluntarily?"

He thrust his fingers through his hair, pushing it out of his face. "Jason asked him to."

"Why?"

"He remembered having the gun. Remembered where the bodies were."

She pressed her tongue hard against her teeth,

absorbing that. "Anything else? Like actually *using* the gun?"

"He turned himself in for murder, Hayley."

"And that doesn't strike you as odd for a man you say is trying to get away with it?"

He shoved his hands through his hair again. "Hell yes, it strikes me as odd!" He paced to the door and back again. "But no more odd than his leading us straight to him in the first place by using a known alias!"

"I want to talk to him. To Jason."

His jaw clenched. "He doesn't want to see you. That's why Tristan told *me*. So I'd keep you from going to the sheriff's station."

It wasn't the first time she'd ever had a patient turn away from her. But it was the first time in such a critical situation. "I want to hear that from Jason."

"Doc—"

"He didn't try to hurt me when we spent hours alone together during our sessions," she interrupted. "He's certainly not going to do anything locked in a jail cell! Whether you like it or not, the man is still my patient."

He watched her from beneath hooded eyes. "And when he tells you he did it? He killed his partners?"

"Then you'll be secure in the knowledge that you were right all along."

His lips twisted. "I didn't *want* to be right. I wanted you to be *safe*."

She held out her arms at her sides. "Do I not look safe?" Because he couldn't possibly say otherwise, she turned and started up the stairs. "How'd Tristan know you were here, anyway?"

"Because as good at disappearing and surveillance as I am, he's got others even better."

She stopped and looked down at him. "That does not make me feel better. This is tiny little Weaver. Stuff like that doesn't belong here." She flexed her fingers around the banister. Her heart was suddenly thumping hard in her chest. "Will you be here when I get back?"

He started up the stairs. "I'll go with you."

Her breath slid out of her. Her mind was swirling, but the only thing that came to her lips was a faint "okay."

He reached her and unpeeled her clenched fingers from the banister. "Better move, Doc. This is a federal case. The sheriff will only have him for a short while."

And you?

The words hung in her mind, but she couldn't make herself ask them. Without Jason's case hanging between her and Seth, would she have him only for a short while, too?

Chapter Eleven

Only two officers were inside the sheriff's station when they arrived. The dark-haired sheriff, Max Scalise, personally escorted Hayley back to the holding cells while Seth cooled his heels in Max's office.

"Tristan warned me you might come," Max said as they went.

"I'm surprised he's not here, too."

"He was. He'll be back."

She knew the urge to warn Seth was childish. He was a grown man who didn't want or need protection from her, even if she was in a position to offer it. Which she wasn't.

Still, she had to concentrate harder than she should have to keep moving forward instead of back. Their footsteps sounded hollow in the empty, tiled corridor. "I appreciate you not trying to stop me from seeing Jason."

"Known you long enough now to know that would be pointless." Max stopped outside the door sectioning off the holding cells without opening it. "I'm allowing it only because you've always helped whenever my department's needed you," he said quietly. "McGregor hasn't asked to see you. In fact, he's stated pretty plainly that he doesn't want to."

"I heard. But I'm also concerned about his state of mind."

"So am I," Max said frankly.

"Has he asked for a lawyer?"

The sheriff shook his head.

She sighed. Even if Jason made a full confession, he should still have legal representation. "None of this would be happening in the first place if Hollins-Winword didn't exist," she murmured.

"Pretty sure Tristan has had a few thoughts along those lines himself," the sheriff answered. "They've done a lot of good, though, too."

"I know your wife is involved—"

"Occasionally," he allowed. "Sarah has been involved. In the past. But my point is only to say that there's a lot of history where Hollins-Winword is concerned. Some of it's not pretty. But when you put things on a scale, the good has always outweighed the bad. Not even the agency can save him from murder charges. You ready to go in?" At her nod, Max pushed open the door leading to the holding cells and gestured her through.

Sam, wearing her uniform, was sitting in a chair outside the cells. She was obviously babysitting their only occupant.

Jason.

"You can head on home, Officer Dawson," Max told her.

Sam nodded. Her gaze met Hayley's for a moment before she left.

Jason was lying on the metal bunk affixed to the wall and didn't budge even when Hayley spoke his name.

"I told them to keep you away," he said.

She glanced at the sheriff and then at the door.

Max's lips tightened, but he retreated after Sam, leaving her alone with Jason.

Once the door was closed again, she stepped up to the cell and studied the gaunt man through the bars. "You need to ask for a lawyer, Jason."

He didn't respond.

"Is there anything I can get for you?"

"A noose."

"Suicide's no answer."

"I killed my friends."

She curled her fingers around one of the thick, cold bars. "You remembered?"

"I remember the gun. I remember the blood. Their bodies." He threw his arm over his eyes. "Go away, Doc. You did your job."

"A job I haven't finished unless you remember more details than that." She looked at the closed door behind her and then back at Jason. "One of my sisters is a public defender."

"I don't need a public defender."

"I can ask her to recommend a lawyer for you."

"Stop trying to help me."

"Then start trying to help yourself!"

He finally looked at her. "I'll get a damn lawyer if you'll leave me alone and get...out. Go pick into somebody else's head."

Hayley hesitated. There wasn't anything more she could do. Not without Jason's cooperation. "But you can get word to me if—"

He'd thrown his arm over his face again.

She sighed, hating the feeling of failure inside her. Hating even more her dreadful suspicion that he hadn't remembered actually committing the heinous deed. But she never had a chance to say anything more because the door opened behind her again and a half-dozen men in black suits filed in, jostling her brusquely aside.

"Hayley." The sheriff took her arm, tugging her out of the way and back through the door. "I'm afraid you need to leave. Seth's waiting for you in my office."

She wanted to protest, but the strange man in the lead was flashing a badge and barking orders and the door shut in her face, leaving her alone in the corridor.

When she entered Max's office, she found Seth squared off with Tristan. "The FBI's here already?"

"And a few other agencies," Tristan said. "McGregor's a popular guy with them all right now. They're having a pissing contest over who gets him first."

Her fists clenched. She wanted to reach for Seth but held back. "Are you okay?"

"Are you?"

She nodded, her eyes searching his. "He didn't remember," she said baldly.

Tristan was the one to answer. "He confessed. Provided enough details to place him at the scene."

"Undoubtedly he was. But did he tell you he aimed the gun at his associates and pulled the trigger? Did he tell you that he wanted them dead and made it happen? Or that they were arguing and in the heat of the moment, he lost it?"

Tristan's expression was stony.

Which was answer enough. "Where are they going to take him? What's going to happen to him?"

Seth's hand slid up her back. "He'll have a

hearing. To determine whether the confession is acceptable or not."

"And if it isn't?"

"He'll need a helluva good lawyer either way," Tristan said. "Because their interest in him isn't just because of Jon and Manny. They think he's one degree of separation away from a terrorist group and that's too damn close."

Hayley was horrified. "That's absurd! You have to help him."

"Hollins-Winword can do a lot. And has, often at the government's request. But right now there's a moratorium on information to us where he's concerned. Nobody's talking at all." He jerked his head toward the office doorway. "I don't even know where those suits plan to take him."

"So you're just going to give up?"

"Rumor has it that you wish Hollins-Winword didn't exist."

"Obviously you and the sheriff had a chance

for a quick chat." She wasn't going to apologize for what she'd said about his company. "Whatever my feelings are about it, the agency does exist. So does some of that good that Sheriff Scalise told me about. Keep them from hanging Jason from a tree for something he didn't do."

"Cole's working on it," he said mildly. "But there's nothing we can do right now to keep him here in Weaver."

Hayley raised her hands. "So that's it?"

"That's it for now where Jason is concerned." Proof of that was plain when they heard the sudden commotion in the outer office and looked back to see Jason, arms and legs in shackles, shuffling between two of the suits. The sheriff was following them, looking grim.

Hayley started to go for the door, but Seth scooped his arm around her waist, holding her back. "This isn't the time to get in their way," he murmured against her ear. "Let it go, Doc."

She winced when the outer door slammed

shut after the men left, taking their prisoner with them.

"This is all wrong," she whispered huskily. Her fingertips pressed against Seth's hard forearm. "I know you think he's dangerous, but this is just all wrong."

He sighed and she felt his lips press against her temple. "I'm sorry, Doc."

Tristan cleared his throat. "The same question exists that always existed," he said when they looked his way. "*Somebody* shot Jon and Manny last year. Jason or someone else. But why? Their covers weren't blown. Jason remembers being there. He couldn't have known some of the details he provided otherwise. If some of his memories are returning, what's the likelihood of the rest coming back?"

A wave of tiredness suddenly washed over her. She couldn't imagine how Seth even managed to stay upright. "Pretty likely," she said. "But there's no guarantee. And certainly no timeframe. Even if he remembers exactly the who, when, where and why of what happened in Central America, is there going to be someone who'll believe him? Someone who'll be able to act on it? And act on his behalf?"

"Yes," Tristan said so quickly that some of her tension slid out of her. "So now my next question," he was looking at Seth, "is whether you're going to be around to help me figure that out or not?"

Hayley chewed the inside of her cheek, fresh tension accosting her.

"You tell me," Seth returned after a long moment. "Is there a job for me to come back to?"

"Been a time or two I haven't followed orders." Tristan pushed away from the desk. "We'll talk about it tomorrow afternoon. In the meantime, I'll leave you two to get on with… whatever." He walked out of the office, leaving them alone.

Hayley looked up at Seth. Her cheeks were hot.

"Well." He took her hands in his and brushed his lips over her knuckles. "You heard the man. Let's get on with…whatever."

"Are you going to keep working for him?"

"I don't know." His blue gaze roved over her face. "I don't know what I'm going to do."

His admission made her chest hurt.

"Since last year, I've thought the man killed his partners. Now I'm not so sure. Maybe I'm wrong." He went silent for a moment. "Maybe I am wrong about what happened to my old man, too."

She wrapped her arms around his wide shoulders. Considering that Hollins-Winword's significant resources hadn't yet resolved the mystery in Central America, she shouldn't be surprised that Seth hadn't been able to use them to shed light on his father's death so long ago. "You were eighteen and alone when that happened. Losing him had to have been devastating. But it was out of your control. Don't blame yourself for that. And don't blame yourself about Jason, either. Everyone suspected him."

"And he had no means to defend himself." Seth's hands rubbed down her arms. "Except for you."

"I didn't accomplish anything. Those people still took him out of here in chains." She pressed her cheek against his. "So I get to live with that."

"You don't want me blaming myself, then you're not gonna get away with blaming yourself. Deal?" He slid his palms down the seat of her jeans.

"Deal," she whispered.

"Good." His lips brushed over hers. "Now, let's get out of here and get on with...whatever." His mouth covered hers and she pushed all her questions about the future out of her mind.

Right now she had the present.

And the present was him.

* * *

"This is not real bacon, Doc."

Hayley hid her smile against her coffee mug and raised her eyebrows at Seth. They were sitting together at the kitchen island and even though it had been close to noon by the time they finally rolled out of bed, Seth had said he was in the mood for bacon and eggs.

So that's what she'd fixed.

"It's not a figment of your imagination," she said.

He gave her a dry look and finished off the crispy piece of turkey bacon. "I like the stuff that actually comes from a pig," he drawled.

She shrugged. "I didn't have any stuff from a *pig* in the fridge."

"We're gonna have to figure something out about this whole meat thing." He shook his head dolefully, but the amusement in his eyes gave him away. "Turkey has its place. On the Thanksgiving table."

She felt a little lurch inside, hoping she wasn't prematurely reading a future into his words. "You didn't even notice it was turkey bacon at first," she countered, picking up his empty plate.

He caught her around the waist and pulled her down onto his lap when she turned to carry the plate to the sink. "I noticed. I was just too hungry to complain about it."

"You're always hungry," she pointed out.

"Well, I am now." His hand slid inside her robe and covered her breast. "Let's go back to bed."

She laughed softly and rubbed her hand over his bare chest. "We spent the morning *in* bed." And she had Gretchen to thank for successfully rearranging her appointment schedule that morning so they could.

"Yeah, but sleepin' doesn't—" He broke off when the doorbell rang. "You don't want to answer that."

She didn't. She wanted to sit there on Seth's lap while he did wicked things with his hands, and then she wanted to go back upstairs, yank off the clean jeans she'd filched from Casey's closet for him to wear and do some wicked things to him.

But the doorbell rang again insistently. "I'll get rid of whoever it is." She brushed her mouth against his, shimmying out from his grasp. "Just hold that thought."

"I'd rather hold you." He pushed off the barstool and followed her to the front door, looking through the peephole before she could. "Sugarnuts," he muttered. "Might want to get some clothes on, Doc."

She couldn't help but smile over his use of the parentally approved curse from her childhood. "Who is it?"

"Your grandmother."

Alarm shot through her, and she snatched the lapels of her robe together as if Vivian could see through the door. "How do you know my grandmother?"

"I don't. But I know she's the lady living in your house."

"I can hear you talking through the door." Vivian's voice was muffled.

She cringed. "Then you know how surprised I am at your visit," she responded as she pulled open the door.

Vivian's bright eyes went from Hayley's robe to Seth's bare chest. "Well, well, well. I guess you've learned how to stay warm at night."

Hayley was mortified but Seth actually chuckled. "This is Seth Banyon," Hayley said dutifully. She didn't know how to describe him, so she didn't try. Particularly when Vivian had already drawn her own conclusions. "Seth, my grandmother, Vivian Archer Templeton."

Vivian held out her hand. "A pleasure."

"The pleasure's mine, ma'am." Seth turned her hand in his and dropped a kiss on the back of it. "Now I see where Hayley gets her beautiful brown eyes."

Hayley's cheeks warmed.

She was fairly certain that Vivian's did, too, though it was hard to tell beneath the rouge she'd generously rubbed on her cheeks.

"Come in," Hayley invited. She was supposed to be pleased about her grandmother getting out and about, but just then, she wished Vivian had chosen to stay holed up at her house with Montrose. "What are you doing here? For that matter, how'd you even know I was here?"

"Your secretary, of course." Vivian clutched her old-fashioned handbag against her waist and strode into the house, looking curiously around her. "Mr. Bumble's been telling me about the excitement at the sheriff's station last night."

"Bubba," Hayley explained in answer to Seth's frown. "From Ruby's."

"Right." He jerked his thumb toward the stairs. "Shirt."

He headed upstairs and Hayley followed barefoot after Vivian. "What did he tell you?"

"That you and your young man were there at all hours. Along with a few dozen vehicles with federal license plates." She sent Hayley an arch look. "Evidently, you've been doing more than house sitting. I thought he'd left town."

She had no intention of telling her grandmother what all had transpired in the past twenty-four hours. "He returned." She tightened the sash on her robe again and pulled out a chair from the table for Vivian to sit, but her grandmother had already spotted Casey's violin and lifted it tenderly from the shelf.

"Good. Now I can decide for myself if he's good enough for you."

"Seth's good enough for anyone."

"Ah." Vivian's thumb strummed gently over the strings. "You *do* like him."

She was in love with him.

But that wasn't something she felt ready to tell her grandmother. It wasn't something she was ready to tell Seth, for that matter.

"What is his background? Does he have people?"

"Grandmother, his background doesn't matter any more than mine does."

"You called me Grandmother," Vivian said.

"Oh." She hadn't even realized. "I'm sorry."

"No." Vivian looked pleased. "Don't be. I think I like it."

Hayley smiled. "I think I like it, too."

Vivian held the violin close to her ear, looking lost in reminiscence. "You're right, of course, about backgrounds. Old habits are just hard to break." She set the violin back on the shelf. "Especially for an old crone like me."

"You're not a crone."

Vivian chuckled. "I'm certainly not a maiden." She sat in the chair at the table and tugged at her chenille jacket. "Anyway, after reviewing the few houses around that are available for sale, I've decided we'll have to build. I've found a few properties that might be suitable."

"Already?"

"At my age there's no time for dilly-dallying." She opened her purse and pulled out a few folded sheets of paper. "I want your opinion before I move forward."

Hayley unfolded the documents and glanced at the acreage listings. "This is probably the best one," she said of the second page. "It's closer to town."

"Yes." Vivian took the paper and studied it. "My Realtor said Squire Clay owns it," she said in a casual tone.

Hayley smiled at the mention of Casey's cattle-ranching grandfather. "He or a member of his family owns most of the land around here. Kind of surprised he's parting with any of it, actually."

"Everyone has their price." Vivian folded the papers but she didn't put them back in her purse. "I'm meeting with an architect this afternoon. I imagine Mr. Ventura will have an opinion about the suitability of the properties, also." Her gaze went past Hayley to Seth as he entered the room. He'd put on one of Casey's vividly patterned shirts, which stretched nearly to its breaking point over his shoulders.

"There's a Rolls-Royce parked out front," he said, looking vaguely shell-shocked.

"Have you driven one?" Vivian asked.

His lips twisted a little. "No, ma'am. Not on my salary."

"I still can't believe she managed to get something like that even delivered here," Hayley said.

"As I said. Everyone has a price." Vivian stood and smiled winningly at Seth. "You can take my granddaughter and me to dinner this evening and have a spin behind the wheel."

"Montrose still not cooking for you?"

Vivian dismissed Hayley's question with a wave of her hand. "He's still in a snit. He'll get over it when I dangle a newly built chef's kitchen in front of his nose." She lifted her eyebrows at Seth. "Well, young man?"

"It'd be my pleasure to escort you ladies to dinner."

Vivian's smile was pure satisfaction. "Preferably someplace with tablecloths this time."

"The only place I know of with tablecloths is in Braden," Hayley warned. "China Palace."

"Fine, fine," Vivian said. "I'm not afraid of Braden, dear," she said as she headed out of the room. "I'll expect you by six."

Seth didn't speak until they heard the front door close after her. "A Rolls-Royce." He shook his head. "That's a fancy car."

"Suits her fancy tastes," Hayley said. "I'm glad she asked you to drive, though. She nearly took out a light pole in town the other day. She wants to hire someone to drive for her, and that can't come soon enough." She unfolded the acreage listings Vivian had left behind and nudged them toward him. "She wants to buy one of these and build a house, too."

He glanced over them, his expression suddenly unreadable. "Think anyone around Weaver has ever had a private driver?"

"Not one who sat behind the wheel of a Rolls-Royce."

Then Hayley leaned over and hooked her arm around his neck and kissed his stubbly jaw. "You still interested in…not sleeping?"

He shoved the papers aside and pulled her right off her chair and onto his lap. "What do you think?"

That evening, they stopped at Hayley's house to pick up Vivian and exchange Hayley's little sedan for the Rolls-Royce, which was, once again, parked haphazardly on the curb.

Hayley knew that Seth had met with Tristan. But he hadn't offered any clue about whether he was going to continue working for Hollins-Winword. She didn't know what he'd do once Casey and Jane returned in a few days and Hayley was back living at home again.

In short…she just didn't know.

And nothing in her *P*, *h* or *D* was helping her resolve that fact.

When her grandmother came out of the house, she was wearing a deep red suit and matching lipstick that made her complexion look pale. "Are you feeling all right?" Hayley asked.

"Of course." Vivian dismissed her granddaughter's concern and handed Seth the key. "I'm sure you want that. Every man I've ever known always wants the car key. Even back in the day when I *liked* driving, my husband Sawyer always wanted the keys." She let Seth help her into the front passenger seat while Hayley took the rear.

"Funny," Seth commented after he'd sat down behind the wheel. "Been all over the world, but

I've only ever heard of two people named Sawyer, right here in Weaver."

Hayley was barely listening. She was busy running her hand over the supple leather seat. "That's right. Tristan's brother's name is Sawyer, too. Hadn't even thought about it. Holy cow. Literally. Holy…cow. This leather is *amazing*."

"I think she likes it, Mrs. Templeton," Seth said dryly.

"Call me Grandmother, dear."

Hayley looked up in surprise and caught Seth's blue eyes watching her in the rearview mirror.

Heat ran up under her skin until she finally looked away.

Her fingers drifted over the fancy armrest beside her seat, and to her bemusement, a tray smoothly unfolded in Vivian's seatback, displaying a screen.

Fancy car. Fancy chef. Fancy fortune. Her grandmother was offering it all and Hayley didn't want any of it. The only thing she wanted was sitting in the driver's seat with inscrutable eyes.

She stifled a sigh and looked out the side window. Seth made some adjustments to his seat, drove off the curb and headed through town, earning surprised looks from everyone they passed.

That hadn't changed even when they reached Braden an hour later. Hayley sat forward to give Seth directions to the restaurant, but Vivian said she wanted to drive by Carter's and David's houses first.

"Just to see where they live," she added crisply. "I have no desire to stop."

So Hayley tamped down her reservations and gave the directions first to her uncle's house. "He's a pediatrician," she told Seth as he slowly cruised by the two-story house. "His practice is right next door." There were no cars or signs of life outside either of the buildings and Hayley wondered if Vivian was disappointed.

When they drove by her parents' house, they met the same results.

"That's the house where I grew up." Hayley pointed out the upstairs window on the side of the house when Seth rolled to a stop on the street. "That was my bedroom."

"Ever sneak out at night?"

She snorted. "Please. I was much better behaved than that. I think Archer might have done so a few times, and I know the Trips did. Are you sure you don't want to stop and go in?"

"Quite." Vivian sounded more than certain. "The last thing I want ruining our evening together is a dose of your father's judgment. Take me to this China Palace of yours. I hope they serve a decent cocktail."

Fortunately, Hayley knew that they did.

When they arrived at the restaurant, the parking lot was crowded for a Thursday evening and there was a line of people waiting outside the door.

Seth let the women off in front of the entrance and drove down the street until he found a spot. By the time he returned, Hayley had obtained a spare chair for her grandmother to use and a waiter was collecting their order for drinks while they waited.

"Tom Collins." Vivian folded her hands in her lap atop her small leather purse and toyed with her rings. "You *can* make a Tom Collins, can't you?"

The waiter looked like a kid in the white shirt and black jeans that all the servers wore. He gulped a little at the look she fastened on him. "Yes, ma'am. I, um, I think we can." He looked quickly at Hayley.

"I'll just have white wine. The house white will be fine."

"Sure you don't want a cosmopolitan?" Seth asked. His dimple flashed.

"I think I'll pass," Hayley assured him dryly.

"Your granddaughter was tanked on cosmos

the night we met," Seth told Vivian and Hayley nearly choked.

"Seth!"

"Never underestimate the persuasive powers of a good cocktail," Vivian said. She gave a small smile. "How do you think a violin-maker's daughter caught the son of a steel magnate?"

"Vivian!"

Her grandmother stood up and smoothed her jacket. "Don't act so shocked, Hayley. People have been people since the dawn of time. Your generation didn't invent sex. You just think you did. Now, if you'll excuse me, I'm going to the ladies' room."

The crowd standing in line seemed to miraculously part to make way for her as she entered the restaurant.

Seth laughed softly. "She's something else."

"Yes."

"You're not smiling about it."

Hayley grimaced. She should have known not to bring Vivian to Braden. The town was twice the size of Weaver, but that still left it too small for comfort.

She looked up at Seth. “That’s because I just saw my dad and stepmother sitting inside.”

Chapter Twelve

"What was I thinking?" She wanted to tear out her hair. "My parents love this place as much as I do."

"So go say hello," he suggested calmly.

"Right." She tugged down the hem of her black T-shirt. The path cleared for Vivian had closed up again, cutting off Hayley's view of Carter and Meredith. "Of course. Just go and say hello. How bad can that be?" She imagined black crows cackling and wondered if it were true that psychologists were all a little crazy.

The waiter had returned, bearing a tray heavy with drinks that he was delivering to more people than just Hayley and her party. When he handed her the wineglass, she nearly snatched it out of his hand and gulped down half of it.

"Dutch courage," she muttered in answer to Seth's raised eyebrows.

"Really a good thing you're sticking to wine," he drawled. He took the beer he'd ordered, as well as Vivian's drink. "Come on. Meet the enemy head-on, Doc."

"I don't want to think of my father as the enemy. Bad enough that he called me that once. 'The Enemy.' Because I was letting Vivian stay with me." She looked at him. "Right before that night at Colbys, actually."

"Explains a lot." He took a pull of beer and then left it on Vivian's vacated chair before grabbing Hayley's hand. "Come on. I want to meet them."

She swallowed another gulp of wine and let

him lead her through the crowd. Once they were inside the restaurant, he nudged her in front of him. "Where are they?"

She latched her fingers through his. "Dad'll be perfectly polite until he realizes his mother is here. Just want to give you fair warning."

"Think I can handle it," Seth said mildly. "Stop stalling."

Was she?

She blew out a breath because she probably was.

Squaring her shoulders, she walked over to where they were sitting at a small round table and fastened a cheerful smile on her face. Only the presence of Seth's hand in hers kept her from tucking her tail and whisking Vivian out of there before they made a scene.

She took the easy route first, touching Meredith's sleeve to get her attention. "Hi."

"Honey!" Meredith's eyebrows shot up and she yanked Hayley forward into a delighted hug.

"What a lovely surprise! Why didn't you let us know you were going to be in town?"

Hayley glanced toward the hallway that led toward the restrooms and saw no sign yet of Vivian. "It was pretty spur-of-the-moment."

Her dad had risen and seemed to be more interested in giving Seth the eagle eye than paying much attention to Hayley when she gave him a tentative hug. He patted her back. "And this would be…?"

"My…my friend, Seth Banyon." She waved her hand as she introduced them. "My parents, Meredith and Carter Templeton."

Seth stuck out his hand toward her father. "Sir."

Carter's demeanor didn't soften, but he returned the handshake. "Seth."

Meredith gave Hayley a meaningful look. Rather than shake Seth's hand, though, she hopped off her chair and pulled him down to kiss his cheek. "I am so pleased to meet you."

He looked a little bemused as he straightened. Hayley could hardly blame him. Meredith tended to have that effect on people.

"Carter, pull up a few chairs from somewhere," Meredith ordered. "Hayley and I are just going to powder our noses." Not waiting for a response, she plucked the wineglass from Hayley's hand and set it on their table. "Your timing is perfect," she said as she dragged Hayley toward the hallway with a determination that belied her petite size. "We haven't ordered yet."

As soon as they were away from the table, though, she stopped. "That's him, isn't it? The special one?"

Hayley nodded. As much as she wanted to talk about Seth with her mom, she was counting her breaths before Vivian appeared. "He is. But, uh, we're not here alone. Vivian's with us."

Meredith's lips rounded. "Oh. *Oh.*" She spread her hands. "Where is she?"

"In the ladies' room."

"Okay." Meredith turned with a flounce and the faint tinkle of bells from her ankle and continued toward the red door marked with a gold *W*. "We'll just take this one step at a time, shall we?" She gave a determined smile and pushed open the door.

Hayley, topping her by a head, saw the same thing that she did and her stomach hollowed out.

Vivian, laying prone on the Oriental rug just inside the door.

Meredith whirled and pushed Hayley toward Vivian. "I'll get help."

"Grandmother." Hayley fell down on her knees next to Vivian. Her grandmother was breathing, but her face was ashen, the rouge that Hayley had thought too heavy earlier now standing out like clown makeup. Hayley grabbed her grandmother's handbag and quickly used it to elevate her feet. "Come on, Vivian. Can you hear me?"

Vivian's eyelids fluttered but didn't open.

Behind her, the door opened and Hayley

scrambled out of the way, looking up to see Seth. Meredith and her father were on his heels. Seth dropped down on the other side of Vivian. "Breathing?" He checked her pulse and listened for himself without waiting for an answer. "Loosen her collar."

Hayley's fingers shook as she unfastened several buttons. She was loosening the belt cinched around Vivian's waist when she suddenly moved.

"What's going on?" Vivian's voice was faint but still managed to contain a demand. "Oh, dear God, get me *off* this floor."

Seth's teeth flashed. "That a girl," he said and carefully helped her up until she was in a sitting position. "Not too fast, though. Looks like you fainted, sweetheart." He rubbed her hands gently and color quickly began returning to Vivian's face. "You do much of that?"

"Templetons do not faint," Vivian muttered. She freed one of her hands and grasped Hayley's. "Most particularly on a bathroom floor. It's simply not done. Get me up."

"Let's just wait a few minutes," Hayley urged. "Are you dizzy? Did you hurt anything when you fell?"

"My dignity," Vivian said.

"*Has* this happened before, Mrs. Templeton?" There wasn't much room left in the small area, but Meredith somehow managed to squeeze in.

"Vivian, this is Meredith. My—"

"I know who she is," Vivian said, managing a shred of impatience despite her condition. "You have pictures of your family all over your little cottage."

She struggled to get up and Seth helped her to her feet, keeping his arm around her as she focused somewhat unevenly on Meredith. "Hayley says you're a lovely person, Meredith, and I have no reason to doubt her. Though I question your judgment in choosing my son, I have come to realize that even the worst of us can somehow manage to find someone to love us. Wouldn't have had my dear Arthur if not for that."

"Even now you can't find something nice to say," Carter said from the doorway.

Vivian peered at Carter. "Good to see you too, son. I'm disinheriting you, by the way."

Meredith just blinked, not saying a word. Hayley could hardly blame her. This was the first time her stepmother had met Vivian and, as usual, her grandmother was living up to form. "I'm sure she doesn't mean that, Dad."

Mother and son spoke at the same time.

"I most certainly do."

"I never wanted the money anyway."

Meredith's wary gaze met Hayley's.

"Perhaps this isn't the place to discuss it," Seth suggested.

Vivian lifted her chin and closed her eyes for a moment, swaying a little. Seth immediately gave her a supporting arm again.

"Vivian." Hayley nervously stepped closer, too. "Are you feeling faint again?"

"No." She opened her eyes and focused on Meredith. "To answer your question, dear, yes. I've fainted before." She looked at Hayley. "To answer your question before you ask it, yes, I know why I fainted. Thanks to this thing in my head," she waved at the back of her neck. "I'm told it may happen more frequently as my time nears."

She ignored Hayley's frown and looked at her son. "That should finally put you at ease, Carter. To know the world will soon be free of the mother you so hate." She stepped away from Seth and stopped in front of Carter, barely coming up to his shoulders. "I wanted to give you the world, but none of you would take it."

His expression was tight. "How could we, when nothing you ever did came without strings? You didn't care about the world that any of us wanted. You only cared about the world that you thought we should want."

"Well." Vivian reached up and patted his cheek as if he were eight instead of fifty-eight. "You're right. I wanted to tell you I was sorry for being a terrible mother. You, being the perfect son that you are, wouldn't allow me even that." The lines on her face stood out.

Carter's jaw worked. Then he spun on his heel and walked away.

Meredith bit her lip. "Mrs. Templeton—"

"Oh, call me Vivian," she said wearily. "Templeton's a name I should have lost the privilege of using many, many years ago."

Meredith tentatively touched her mother-in-law's sleeve. "He's looked at the photo album every day since Hayley brought it by. He's just not ready to admit that to you. According to David's wife, neither is he."

Vivian's eyes moistened. "Thank you, dear.

You should probably go after him so he doesn't worry you've become tainted by me."

"We're going to meet again." Meredith's encouraging look encompassed both Hayley and Vivian. "It's bound to get better each time."

The restroom door opened and a teenaged girl stopped short at the sight of them. Particularly Seth. Her mouth rounded in an "oh" and she quickly backed out again. Meredith followed.

"Well, that was fun," Vivian said. "Where's my Tom Collins?"

"Vivian," Seth said quietly. "Cut the crap."

Hayley went into one of the stalls and yanked off a hank of toilet paper. She blew her nose and washed her hands. If she'd had to work with a family like hers in her practice, she would have suggested they'd benefit from intense therapy. "You," she told her grandmother, "have some explaining to do."

"That may be true, but I'm not doing it in the ladies' room." Vivian refastened the buttons at her neck and patted her hair. Despite her authoritative tone, though, she held on tightly to Seth's arm as he escorted her back into the restaurant.

Not surprisingly, Meredith and Carter hadn't returned to their table. It had already been cleared for the couple who'd replaced them.

"We should get her back to Weaver," Hayley whispered to Seth. "Take her to the hospital."

"My hearing is perfectly fine, missy." Vivian gave Hayley a stern look. "And there's nothing they can tell me at the Weaver hospital that I don't already know. I got woozy and didn't sit down quickly enough for it to pass. So I fainted. Simple enough. Now—" she looked at the line still leading out of the restaurant "—where's the maître d'? I'm sure the usual financial persuasion will produce a table for us. Once I eat I'll be fine."

The restaurant had a nice cloth on each table, but the teenaged girl wielding a pencil and a notepad at the hostess station wasn't exactly a maître d'.

"Until the next time you faint," Seth said.

"Which could be another six months away or tomorrow," Vivian returned. "I'm *fine* and I want to eat."

The last thing Hayley wanted was to see Vivian wind herself up even more. "We'll find you some food," she soothed. Her own appetite had gone the way of the dinosaurs and she was wishing they'd never left Weaver—with the hospital only minutes away—in the first place. "But maybe we should go somewhere that will be quicker."

Seth transferred Vivian's arm to Hayley's. "Hold tight." He worked his way to the hostess station.

"You need to marry him," Vivian said. "But do it quickly, before I'm gone."

"Grandmother!"

"Well? You want to, don't you?"

Hayley's own head felt as if it was buzzing inside. "I haven't given it any thought," she lied.

"Hmm." Vivian clearly didn't believe her. "Next time you're alone with him, wear a dress," she advised. "Never underestimate the power of a pretty girl in a dress. Makes the man feel very...manly."

A worried, rueful laugh rose in Hayley's throat. All too easily, she remembered Seth's comment about her skirt the afternoon they'd gone to the park together. "I'll keep that in mind. But I don't want to hear you talking about being gone." She pressed her hand over Vivian's. "You're not going to distract me from what just happened here."

"I certainly wish I could." Vivian smiled suddenly. "Ah, look. Seth found us a table."

Naturally. It seemed he could accomplish anything he set his mind to.

He took Vivian's arm again and escorted her slowly toward the table that the hostess had miraculously produced. Judging by the wide-eyed expression on the girl's face as she looked at Seth, it wasn't hard to guess there'd been no need for any financial incentive. All he'd needed to do was smile.

He helped Vivian with her chair and leaned over. "You're getting your way right now, Vivian." His Texas drawl seemed more pronounced than ever. "But after we're done, you *are* going to see a doctor. No arguments. Got that?"

Vivian sent Hayley an arch look. "Of course, dear," she said. "Anything you say."

The hospital, ignoring her slew of imperious protests, admitted Vivian.

"Tests." She spit out the word like a curse as she sat in her hospital bed wearing a blue dotted gown that swamped her narrow shoulders. "I had plenty of tests with my own doctors."

"Yet you mentioned none of them to me," Hayley pointed out. "For six…no, seven months now, not one word."

"There was no point. My doctors in Pittsburgh couldn't do anything about this tumor growing inside my head. If they can't, nobody can. Now go on." She waved her hands at Hayley and Seth. "Take her home, Seth. I don't need the two of you hovering over me looking like you're afraid I'll die if you blink." She closed her eyes, resting her head back against the pillows propped behind her. "I detest hovering."

"We'll come back in the morning," Seth said, seeming to miss the quick glance Hayley couldn't help giving him. "Don't give the doctors here too hard a time, hmm?"

Vivian pressed her lips together. "We'll see." She opened her eyes. "And don't tell Montrose I'm here. The man will have a hissy fit."

Despite everything, Hayley couldn't help but smile a little over hearing the word "hissy" come out of her grandmother's mouth. "He'll be worried when you don't come back tonight."

"Tell him I'm out finding husband number five. He'll believe that." She closed her eyes again. *"Go."*

"She'll be fine," the middle-aged nurse who'd been standing nearby assured them. "We'll look after your grandmother."

"Thanks."

Seth nudged Hayley into the corridor outside Vivian's private room and wrapped his arms around her.

Hayley held on to him. "All this time she's been sick and I didn't know. How could I not know?"

"The important thing is that you know now." He kissed her forehead. "Come on. I've had drill sergeants who were less intimidating than Vivian."

"I doubt you're afraid of anything." She let him turn her toward the exit.

“I’m not real thrilled about snakes.”

She raised her eyebrows, smiling a little. “My brother Arch had a pet snake when we were kids.”

Seth grimaced. “No accounting for taste.”

“We didn’t have dogs or cats because Meredith’s allergic to them.”

“That does explain your skill with a dog leash,” he said dryly. “But a snake was the solution?” He shook his head.

“For Archer it was.” She waved as they passed a nurse she knew, coming on for her night shift. “I had fish. The Trips had a turtle.”

“And Rosalind?”

“She had a dog. She didn’t live with us full-time. She just came once a month for the weekend. The rest of the time she was with her dad, Malcolm, in Cheyenne.” They left the antiseptic brightness of the hospital building for the dark Weaver night. “You didn’t have a chance to bring back your truck from Braden.”

"Guess I'll have to make do with driving your granny's hunk o' junk." He smiled. "For tonight, anyway. Wanna make out in the back? The headliner has lights in it that look like stars."

"I noticed." She chewed the inside of her cheek. Weaver had plenty of stars in the sky. The real kind.

"Not the response I was looking for, Doc." He settled his hand on the small of her back as they crossed the parking lot toward the vehicle that looked like a gleaming jewel sitting among a field of pickup trucks.

"She wants to leave it all to me," Hayley admitted abruptly. "All of it. She even changed her will."

His hand slid away from her back. "I see."

"I don't want any of it." She gestured at the extravagant car in front of them. "Not even a car with a starry-lit back seat."

"Then don't take it."

Hayley threw out her arm toward the hospital. "You've seen what she's like. She's going to get her way somehow. According to my father, money *ruled* her life and ruined theirs. She lost her Arthur. Now I find out she has a brain tumor. Considering all that, it's perfectly understandable that she'd want to mend her relationship with her sons. But that doesn't change the years that came before." She shook her head. "I don't want that burden. Not any of it."

"You wouldn't let money change you, Doc."

"How do you know?" she challenged. "How can any of us know what—" she waved her hand at the vehicle "—*that* does to a person? That car's worth more than most people make in a year. In two years. Three. And she acquired it at the snap of her fingers."

"Because I know you. You're already smart. Already beautiful. You were out of my league from the get-go and money's not—"

Her head reared back. "What do you mean out of your league?"

"It doesn't matter. The point—"

"It does matter."

He frowned slightly. "You really want to get into this now?"

"Get into?" She felt something yawning open inside her. "I think we are already there."

His shoulders rose and fell and his hands went to his hips. "You're Dr. Hayley Templeton," he said evenly. "I can't even claim to be a security guard. Don't know if I even want the job Tristan says I still do have. You've got a Ph-freaking-D and I'm a former army grunt who didn't even stick it out to retirement. I've got only what the army taught me. From the start, you've been so far out of my league, we're not even playing in the same universe."

She breathed carefully, but it was no use. The words just flooded out of her. "I can't believe we're back to that. After everything that's happened, we're back to that. I don't care if you're a security guard! Or if you're an intelligence analyst or the next Double-Oh-Seven! And no amount of money is going to change that." Realization swept over her. "Oh. Right. I'm not the one with a problem about what you do. You're the one with a problem about me. Better yet, with a problem about you."

He didn't deny it. Didn't do anything but stand there, watching her with his inscrutable eyes.

"I just keep reading more into things than I should with you. I wanted to believe everything that's happened meant something...more." She'd wanted to believe the way he'd touched her meant something more.

"It did mean something."

"Finishing the mission where Jason was concerned?" Aching inside, she stared into his face. "Were you really hoping he'd give you a reason to shoot him? To picture your father's partner's face in place of Jason's when you pulled the trigger?" She knew the words were unforgiveable even as she said them. Which just proved that she had more of Vivian in her than she thought.

"Hayley—"

"Don't." It was too much on top of too much. Vivian. Jason. Knowing she was in love while he'd just been doing his job. "I should have paid more attention to your words early on. 'We both wanted to get laid.'"

His jaw looked tight. "You know it's more than that."

"Do I? I'm in love with you, Seth." Saying the words shouldn't have hurt so much. "I. Love. You. Not what you do. Not how much education you had or didn't have or how many zeroes are on your paycheck. You."

She gestured at the car. "You should drive it while you can." Her voice felt raw. "You could even be Grandmother's chauffeur. It might suit your misguided perception about yourself better than any other career ever could." She turned on her heel and started walking.

"Where are you going?"

"Home." She didn't look back.

Chapter Thirteen

"Here." A wrinkled hand with diamonds on nearly every finger appeared in Seth's side vision and set a long-neck bottle of beer in front of him. "You look like you're in need of another."

Seth looked from the two empties in front of him to Vivian. "Last time I saw you, you were in a hospital bed complaining about having tests." And followed on the heels of that, Hayley had washed her hands of him.

A week later and he was still feeling run through.

"And the results were what I said they would be. So it was a complete waste of time."

She didn't ask if he minded company.

Which he did.

She just commandeered the barstool next to him.

"This is an atrocious place." She plucked a bar napkin from the basket in front of them and unfolded it on the scarred bar top before placing her handbag on it.

"Yup." She'd given him a cold beer, so he twisted off the cap and pitched it onto the floor where it could mingle with dozens of others just like it. "Don't think I'd be real welcome at Colbys these days." Casey was back at work after his honeymoon. He'd been showing unusual tact, all things considered. Seth doubted his wife, Hayley's best friend and Colbys' owner, would be so forgiving.

"Hmm." Vivian pushed an ashtray brimming

with cigarette butts off to the side. "Aren't there no-smoking laws?"

"Does it look like they care?" He gave a pointed look around the dive bar. Jojo's was located as far out on the edge of Weaver as it was possible to get. "What are you doing here, Vivian? How'd you find me?" He gave her a sharp look. "Is Hayley okay?"

"Yes to the last. Money to the second. And if you don't know the answer to the first, maybe you're not smart enough for my granddaughter after all."

"Nice way with the sweet talk."

"Oh, you want sweet talk." Vivian looked amused. "Men never change. The older I get the more I realize that." She thumped her hand twice on the bar to get the bartender's attention. "You there. I'll have a Tom Collins."

The bartender grunted. "Told you already, lady. We got beer, whiskey and gin. Mixin' 'em together in a glass is as fancy as it gets."

Vivian sent Seth a look. “I should open a proper club. Montrose needs a challenge.”

“You’d go out of business in a week. Especially with Montrose.”

“You’ve never even met him.”

“Didn’t need to. Hayley told me enough.” Just saying her name felt like poking at a broken bone with a sharp stick.

“Whiskey,” she told the bartender. “Neat.”

She waited until the heavy-bearded man slid the glass across the bar to her. “Save me from the Wild West,” she muttered and plucked another napkin from the basket. She worked it around the rim of the glass before taking a sip and grimacing. “My father liked whiskey.” She lifted the glass again and tossed back the rest. Then she shuddered once and set the glass down, waving her finger over it.

Looking grumpy, the bartender retrieved the glass and prepared her another.

“Should you be drinking like that?”

"Because I have a tumor squatting in my head?"

Seth almost caught himself smiling. "Yes."

"Seems like as good a time as any to me." She wiped the rim of the fresh drink but didn't down it in one fell swoop this time. "It hasn't gotten worse," she explained. "It's the same miserable, itty-bitty size that it was a year ago in Pittsburgh. If I'm lucky enough to join dear Arthur tomorrow, it's only going to be if I walk in front of a bus. Thank you for asking."

He gave her a look that she ignored.

"Hayley's miserable."

"I'm not discussing her with you, Vivian."

"We're not having a discussion. I'm *informing* you that she is miserable. Not that she says anything, of course. But I can see it in her eyes. I thought you were a smart man, Seth."

"Smart enough not to repeat my pop's mistakes." He started to tap out a cigarette from the pack beside him but stopped. Smoking in front of a woman her age, with a brain tumor no less, was disgusting. He never should have started back up. He'd had the habit kicked once he'd left the service, only indulging on rare occasions.

Like that first night with Hayley, when she'd had to delicately snore off her cosmopolitans in his bed.

He shoved the smoke back into the pack and lifted the beer again.

"He chose a woman out of his reach, too," he said.

"Oh, yes. Roberta Tierney," Vivian mused, lifting her glass to study the contents in the light and ignoring the narrow-eyed look he suddenly gave her. "Of Tierney Textiles before they were taken over years ago by Forco." She swirled the contents of her glass a few times. "Did you know that Jake Forrest, who used to run Forco, lives right here in Weaver?" She shook her head. "Voluntarily goes from running one of the largest textile firms in the country, raising and running thoroughbreds as a hobby, to living out here. If I live to be a hundred, I'll never understand what the *appeal* is here." She laughed lightly and patted his arm. "Of course, we know I'll never live to be a hundred."

"Vivian."

She stopped patting. Her fingertips stabbed into his arm and she gave him a steely look. "Did you really think I wouldn't find out everything I could about you before giving my seal of approval?"

"I'll give you points for fast work, but I don't give a flip about your approval," he said flatly. "Stay out of my business."

"Hayley is my business," she retorted.

"Is that the tack you took with her father? No wonder he's your biggest fan."

"I do like you," Vivian murmured. Her pointed fingernails retreated and she patted his arm again. "You're not afraid to speak your mind. And I like that. Reminds me of dear Arthur."

"Was that his first name? Dear?"

The wrinkles around her eyes deepened and she let out a laugh that sounded a little rusty. "My dear Arthur had a sense of humor, too. I had four husbands," she mused. "I loved two of them. The first. And the last."

"I'm sure you're enjoying your trip down memory lane, but I'm a little busy here."

"Of course you are, dear. Drinking and smoking are fine pursuits."

He exhaled and gave her another look that she blithely ignored. "How did you find out about the Tierneys?"

"Money, my dear." She sipped the whiskey. "I have a very good attorney, to whom I pay very good money, who is very good at such matters. It wasn't difficult. You had a birth certificate, after all, with all of the lines duly completed. Made things quite easy for Stewart this time, actually." She slid Seth a look. "You must not know anything about Hayley if you're comparing my granddaughter to the woman who abandoned you."

"I'm not comparing Hayley to anyone."

"Then you're comparing yourself to your father." She sipped again. "That was a sad business. The way he died."

"Should I suspect that Hayley told you about it, or is that courtesy of more of your money?"

"Hayley has told me nothing. She'd be furious if she knew I was here."

He stared ahead at the dusty wood paneling on the wall on the other side of the bar. "So why are you here?"

"Because I want her to be happy," Vivian said simply. "I haven't accomplished anything that I came to Weaver to do. Neither Carter nor David are speaking to me. Nothing new there, of course. They've had years of practice. As for trying to make amends for my other sins—" She broke off and shook her head. "I want her to be happy," she said again.

"That makes two of us." He sucked on the beer even though he'd lost the taste for it.

"Then what are you doing alone in this dreadful place?"

He set the beer bottle down carefully. "What do I have to offer her?"

"What is it that you think you need to offer her?"

"The world. Which is a little outta the budget on my salary." He found himself pulling out another cigarette and muttered an oath. He squeezed the pack, breaking the cigarettes inside, and pitched it into the overflowing trash can on the other side of the bar.

"Take some advice from an old woman," Vivian said. "Don't try giving someone the world. It never works out." She polished off the rest of her drink. "The only thing that works is giving them your heart. And that doesn't cost a dime." Her voice was tart, but he saw the softness in her brown eyes as she lifted her handbag off the bar to extract some cash. "I learned *that* from dear Arthur. He was a public school teacher. And he was the love of my life."

She dropped the money on the bar and stood, but as soon as she took a step, she seemed to stumble a little and he caught her shoulders. "You're not going to faint, are you?"

"Just too many peanut shells thrown on the floor," she said.

There were plenty of shells, it was true. They crunched under Seth's boots with every step he took, but he still kept hold of her arm, walking her outside the stale building. The Phantom was parked in the dirt parking lot. "You shouldn't be driving."

"I'm not," she assured him. "I hired a driver."

Of course she had. "Vivian, you are…one of a kind."

"Something which Carter and David are grateful for every day."

"That's not what I meant."

She patted his cheek. "I know, dear. But it's always easier to fall back on form than let someone know they matter. Less chance of having one's feelings wounded." She hooked her handbag more firmly in the crook of her arm, smoothed the back of her hair and picked her way across the rutted dirt to the Rolls-Royce.

A teenager Seth didn't recognize climbed out of the vehicle before she got there and opened the door.

Seth couldn't help shaking his head slightly at the odd sight.

Vivian slid into the luxurious car and looked out at him. "I've learned sometimes you have to go back before you can truly go forward. Think about that, Seth, would you?" Without waiting for an answer, she pulled the door closed.

The kid driving the car gave Seth a crooked smile. "Some crazy lady, huh?"

"Yeah." Seth tapped the roof of the car. "Be careful driving her around. She's valuable."

"I know." The boy's Adam's apple bobbed as he went back to the driver's side door. "She is one sweet car," he said before climbing inside.

"I'm not talking about the car," Seth murmured as the vehicle rolled smoothly over the rough dirt.

When it was gone, he went to his truck that looked even worse than usual after sitting next to a Rolls-Royce.

How far back would he have to go before he could go forward?

He pinched the bridge of his nose.

He could go back a week and pretend that he'd never lost his mind and let Hayley walk away from him. If she'd take him back.

But she hadn't been entirely wrong with her accusations. He had wanted to believe McGregor was guilty of killing his partners. He had wanted to make sure he'd pay for it.

Which meant Seth needed to go back a lot

further than just a week. He needed to go back half a lifetime.

One more time.

"How do you know Seth left town?" Sam propped her foot on the park bench beside Hayley and leaned over in a long stretch.

The last thing Hayley wanted to do was go running; instead, she wanted to curl up somewhere and never lift her head again. But she also knew that hiding herself away wouldn't ease the pain inside her. Only time was going to do that, and time passed more quickly when one was busy.

She didn't even need her Ph-freaking-D to know that.

"Because I couldn't stand it anymore and I went to his apartment yesterday," she admitted, yanking the laces of her running shoe into a messy bow. Silence broadcast Sam's surprise loud and clear and Hayley dug her chin into her leg before needlessly retying her shoe for about the fifth time. "Mrs. Carson—the lady who lives in the apartment underneath his—told me. Again. He's been gone for a week."

"Yes, well, she wasn't entirely accurate the first time," Sam pointed out reasonably.

Hayley straightened. She didn't want Sam to sound reasonable. She wanted her friend to sound as outraged as Hayley felt brokenhearted.

"I think I need therapy," she muttered.

"Don't we all?" Sam's smile was wry. She lowered her foot and grabbed Hayley under the arm, dragging her off the bench. "Come on. You put in three miles with me today and I'll treat you to a cinnamon roll over at Ruby's."

"Bribery."

"Whatever works." Sam started jogging in place. "Maybe we can get Jane out this weekend for a girls' night. I haven't seen her since she and Casey got back from their honeymoon and that was two whole weeks ago." She turned and set off on the sidewalk that led around the pavilion.

Hayley fell into place behind her. "I hate jogging," she said.

"I hate vegetables," Sam said without looking back. "Still need to eat 'em. So what do you think? Girls' night out?"

Hayley blew out a noisy breath. "Sure." Anything was better than spending another night alone, wishing she'd never said the things she'd said to him. Wishing that she would have just climbed with him into the back of her grandmother's ridiculous car with the starry headliner. Because taking what he'd offered then would have meant being with him now.

Instead, she had nothing but an empty bed at night and a bald-headed Montrose banging pots and pans with displeasure in her kitchen in the morning.

They'd made it twice around the park before Sam broke the silence. "Heard that Homeland

Security's not interested in McGregor anymore." Her short ponytail bobbed in time to her footsteps.

Hayley sped up enough to draw even with her. "What? How'd you hear that?"

"Went out with Conover last night." She glanced at Hayley. "You know. Adam," she added. "Guard out at—" She waved her hand, not finishing.

Hayley caught Sam's hand and dragged her to a stop. "How much do you know about that?"

"Not as much as you, I'm guessing." Sam immediately began jogging in place again. "Sheriff filled us in on what we needed to know."

"And that's good enough for you?"

Sam lifted her shoulder. "It doesn't just take a village to raise a kid. It takes one to keep the world safely turning, too. Keep moving, girlfriend." She slapped Hayley on the hip of her sweatpants and set off again. "Got two more laps before you're off the hook. Anyway, story is McGregor's confession has also been tossed by a federal judge. Supposedly, too many inaccuracies."

"How do you *know* all of this stuff?"

Sam's smile flashed. "I haven't been walking around in a funk for two weeks." Her feet pounded. "Get the lead out, Templeton. I'm sure Seth knows, but…" Her voice trailed off and she ran in silence for another half a lap before slowing her pace enough to drop back to Hayley's. "You think he'll come back?"

Hayley swiped her arm over her forehead. She was sweating like a fiend, yet Sam looked as if she could keep running forever. "You're not even sweating," Hayley whined.

Sam laughed silently. "Put in more than a couple miles twice a week and you could say the same."

"No, thanks."

"So, do you?"

"Do I what? Dislike you intensely right now? Yes."

"Think he'd come back here if he could?"

What little breath she had seemed to leave her completely. "I don't know. Mrs. Carson didn't offer a suitcase count this time."

"I was talking about McGregor. If his case gets tossed altogether."

Hayley slowed to a stop, leaned over and rubbed the stitch in her side. "I don't know why he would. He's got nothing here to come back to." She peered at her friend through the sweat stinging her eyes. "Why?"

Sam lifted her shoulders. She was still jogging in place, but she didn't meet Hayley's eyes. "Just curious."

"Jason McGregor isn't exactly tall, rich and temporary."

Sam's lips quirked. "I know." Her feet finally stopped moving. "I was on duty the night he turned himself in."

"I remember."

"I just...I don't know. Something about the guy is sorta sticking with me. You know what I mean?"

Hayley blew out a long breath. "I know exactly what you mean." She straightened and tucked her arm through Sam's. "Cinnamon roll. Please. I beg you. And when we're *sitting,* while I indulge myself in a sweet roll drenched in caramel and pecans, you can tell me all about it."

"Dr. Templeton is in?"

"Dr. Templeton is in." They waited while a tractor pulling a load of hay lumbered past. Then they crossed the street, heading for Ruby's just around the block.

"How's Vivian's hunt for the new Templeton estate coming along?"

"How do you think? She hired Beck Ventura as the architect. He'll probably regret it before the house is built. She keeps changing her mind about what she wants."

"What does she want?"

"A palace?"

Sam laughed softly. "Where is she going to build?"

"That remains to be seen," Hayley said. "She wants a piece of land that Squire Clay's got up for sale but she hasn't made an offer yet for some reason." They turned the corner and reached the diner.

"You got new running shoes," Sam observed. "Just noticed."

Hayley lifted the drooping leg of her sweatpants to wiggle her hot pink shoe. "Had to. I was careless for thirty seconds and Moose ate my other ones."

"Bet you're glad Jane's back. That house of theirs is to die for, but that puppy? Sounds like he eats everything in sight."

She immediately thought of Seth. Moose had never tried to chew something he shouldn't when Seth was around. "I miss him."

"The dog?"

"Yeah. Him, too." She followed Sam through the door to the diner and inhaled the heavenly aroma of coffee and cinnamon.

"Well, my friend," Sam said, "Looks like now's your chance to tell him."

"What?"

Sam spread her hands and stepped to one side.

Leaving Hayley standing face-to-face with Seth.

"You shaved," she breathed and immediately turned hot. She hadn't seen him in two weeks. Two long, miserably lonely weeks. And those were the words that came out of her mouth?

His lips tilted in a smile and without the usual blur of dark razor stubble, his dimple fully revealed itself. He rubbed his hand down his jaw, looking vaguely self-conscious. "I did." His eyes ran over her face. "You look—"

"—sweaty," she offered quickly. "Running. I've been running with, um, with Sam." And why, oh, why couldn't she be wearing something presentable like Sam's body-hugging capris and sports bra, instead of her ancient sweats and a faded UCLA T-shirt with a tear on the hem?

"Good," he corrected her. "I was going to say you look good."

She lifted her eyebrows, sticking her fingers through the ripped hem. "I look like something that Moose got hold of." Seth, however, looked as amazing as always in the simplest of blue jeans and an ARMY T-shirt that hugged his shoulders.

"I'm not looking at the clothes."

Her stomach lurched. "I—" Her brain seemed frozen. She didn't know what to say. So all she did was smile weakly and choke out a nervous laugh.

Sam jostled her in the ribs with her elbow. "I'm going to finish my run," she said, widening her eyes at Hayley almost comically. "I'll catch up to you later." She looked at Seth. "Nice to see you back."

Then she trotted out the diner door.

"I came in for cinnamon rolls." Hayley forced out the words as if they'd been the ones on her lips all along.

He held up a white paper sack. "So did I."

"Oh."

"I've got enough to share."

Something inside her chest leapt. "Okay." She moistened her lips and glanced around the diner. Every booth, table and counter stool was occupied. "I don't see anywhere to sit."

"I know a place."

She swallowed and preceded him out the door.

"This will do," he said gruffly the second they were outside the restaurant, and he pushed her against the brick wall, fastening his mouth hungrily over hers.

Her hands fisting in his hair, she kissed him back before she realized what she was doing right there in the middle of Main Street, Weaver, USA. She gasped and shoved him away, pressing the back of her hand to her throbbing lips. "What is wrong with you?"

"Nothing's wrong." He was breathing hard. "But at least now you're not looking at me like you don't know whether to run and hide or hide and run." He bent over and scooped up the paper bag that he'd dropped. "How is Vivian?"

Hayley's legs were trembling and she wished she could blame it on the aborted jog with Sam, but lying to herself had been losing its appeal for a good fourteen days now. "She's decided to build a house. She's bringing her old housekeeper out from Pittsburgh, which has Montrose in a tizzy because they don't get along at all. And why did Mrs. Carson tell me again that you left town?"

In the bright morning sun, Seth's eyes were a blue gleam between his narrowed lashes. "Because I did." He pulled her around to the back of Ruby's, where a table and bench were set up beneath a tree. "Vivian visited me a week ago."

Hayley started.

"Said a few things that got under my skin."

"She has a way of doing that," Hayley said faintly.

"Most importantly, about sometimes needing to go back before you could forward." His gaze bore into hers. "So I did." He pulled a folded envelope out of his pocket and handed it to her.

"What's this?"

"Proof that Marcus killed my father. The original autopsy report was lost a long time ago, but that's a statement from the medical examiner who signed off on it. He's retired now but he kept meticulous records. My father didn't drown. He was dead before he hit the water. The ME confirms there's no way that the injury was accidental."

She gaped and sat on the bench with a plop.

He straddled the bench and sat beside her. "I

wasn't wrong. Marcus paid off the DA to avoid prosecution and took the rest of the money he'd gotten for the sale of the business and booked a flight to Mexico."

"How do you know?"

"With a little help from Hollins-Winword, the DA—he's retired, too—admitted he'd taken the payoff. He decided confessing to that was less painful in the long run than having us dig through every single one of the cases he didn't prosecute over his short, uncelebrated career."

"Seth." She squeezed his hands. "That's wonderful. You were right all along."

"And there's no statute of limitation on murder. Marcus has already been picked up in Mexico. He'll be extradited back here to the United States to face charges."

Hayley's eyes burned. She twined her arms around his neck. "I'm so glad for you," she whispered huskily. "You finished your mission." Before she clung too hard for too long, she sat back.

"I did," he murmured. "Only because Vivian stuck her nose in where it didn't belong. She's not all bad."

Hayley nodded. "She's not all good, either."

"Isn't that human nature, Dr. Templeton?"

Her lips curved upward in a smile but not for long. She swallowed the knot in her throat. "So what are you going to do now? Go back to Texas?"

He shook his head. "There's nothing for me in Texas."

"Won't you want to be there to see Marcus's trial?" She thought about Sam's claim that Jason's trial might never come to pass. "Surely there will be one, won't there?"

"Chances are he'll take a lesser manslaughter plea before it ever gets that far. He's not going to want to take his chances on a murder conviction in Texas, when there are too many witnesses still around to confirm he was the only one on the boat with my father." He turned her hand over and pressed his palm against hers. "What I want is here."

She sank her teeth into the tip of her tongue. "You don't have to say that. I overreacted about Vivian's will and…and all that. I was—"

"—panicking." He cut her off. "I know." His eyes searched hers. "And I do have to say it. What I *want* is here. Everything I want is here. Because you are here." He curled his fingers through hers. "I am never going to feel like I'm good enough for you. That's a fact, Doc, and not one I'm capable of changing. But I'm also not capable of changing the fact that I love you." His fingers tightened.

The tears in her eyes leaked out. "I shouldn't have said what I did. It was…cruel."

He cupped her cheek and brushed his thumb over her tears. "You don't have what it takes to be cruel, Doc. It's not in your DNA." His dimple flashed, quick as lightning in a summer storm and gone just as fast. "But you can fire as straight a verbal shot as anyone I've ever known. And I wouldn't want you any other way."

"So you're going to stay in Weaver?"

"I'm going to stay with you." His eyes searched hers. "Surrender is not a Ranger word." He took her hand and placed it against his heart. "But I'm surrendering everything I have to you. If you'll take me."

Her chest felt as if it would crack. Her lips parted but no words would come.

His thumb brushed down her cheek. "But we're not gonna live with Vivian. I draw the line at some things, and that's one of them. And our kids aren't gonna drive around in Rolls-Royce Phantoms. Not unless they earn 'em themselves."

"Kids?"

His eyes softened, suddenly filled with that unexpected sweetness that had entranced her from the very beginning. "Do you ever think about it?"

She nodded because her throat was too tight for anything else. "I do," she managed to croak.

He brushed her mouth with his. "Keep practicing those words, Doc. You can use them when you marry me. If you want to, that is."

She suddenly laughed through her tears and pulled him close. "I do. I do, I do, I do!"

Epilogue

Two months later to the day, they did.

They were married under the round pavilion in the Weaver Community Park.

The same park where she had first seen him.

Hayley wore a white embroidered satin halter dress that hit just above her ankles. Isabella Clay had miraculously produced it in record time, claiming that it had been easy since she still had Hayley's measurements from the dress she'd worn for Jane's wedding so recently and the style of the dress was similar. Hayley had a hard time believing the task had been all that easy.

Fortunately, Vivian had insisted on paying for the dress and Hayley knew that her grandmother would have made certain Isabella's effort was handsomely rewarded.

Seth wore a black suit and white shirt and was happy to eschew the tie when Hayley suggested it. She knew he disliked them. And even though he'd have happily worn it for her, she'd wanted him to be himself. If he'd have wanted to wear jeans and a T-shirt, she wouldn't have cared.

The wedding wasn't about what they wore.

It was about the commitment that they were making for the rest of their lives.

Jane and Sam were her attendants. Hayley had told them to wear what they chose.

Sam, practical-minded as ever, wore the same dress she'd worn for Jane's wedding. And Jane, equally practical, had chosen to wear Hayley's maid-of-honor dress. She'd had to have it cleaned because there were dirt marks around the hem from the parking lot at Shop-World where Hayley had danced with Seth.

Two of his ranger buddies made it into town in enough time to stand up for him. They looked stunning in their dress uniforms. Which had Sam eyeing them as if they were treats to be devoured but she couldn't decide between them.

Much to Vivian's chagrin—because she'd wanted to hire an entire orchestra as befitted any granddaughter of hers—Casey provided the music, playing his violin. And he did so with such perfect beauty that Hayley saw Vivian wipe a tear as she stared fixedly at the man.

Even Seth noticed, murmuring "Is your grandmother crying?" into her ear when she met him in front of the minister after her father had walked her beneath the pavilion.

"It's the violin music," she whispered back. "My grandfather used to play."

Her father had promised not to make a scene

with her grandmother. At least not on Hayley's wedding day. And even now, after the vows and the rings, Carter managed to limit himself to an occasional glare across the invisible aisle separating the picnic tables where everyone sat.

Despite coming together for a wedding, Carter and his brother were keeping very much to one side of the pavilion. Vivian stayed to the other, sharing her table with Montrose and Gretchen. There were other guests, too. Former clients and friends of Hayley's. Isabella and her husband, Erik, and their adopted son, Murphy. Abby and Sloan McCray. The sheriff and his wife. Even Pam Rasmussen, the sheriff's dispatcher, who was married to Hayley's distant cousin.

Vivian and her sons could sit on opposite sides of the aisle, pretending the other side didn't exist. But there were connective threads webbing out around them whether they liked it or not.

"Do you suppose they'll ever let the past go?" Seth asked, sliding his arm around Hayley's waist. The gold band she'd put on his finger only minutes ago gleamed. She kept getting distracted just from looking at it.

He was her husband. She was his wife.

She glanced at her father. He and David had moved near the wedding cake where Casey and Jane were standing. Vivian was cradling Casey's violin close by. "I don't know. I'm not worrying about it anymore," she said. "It's not up to me to fix them."

"You'll never let it go. You'll always be concerned about the people you love. That's who you are."

"Who I am," she turned into his arms, loving the smile on his face, "is your wife."

"Dr. Hayley Banyon. You're sure you want to change your name?"

"Positive." She dipped her fingertip into his dimple. "I never knew how much I could love someone until I met you."

"You're just saying that because you want to get your hands on me."

She laughed softly. "That's right, Mr. Banyon. It's all about the sex. The very, very good sex. Has nothing whatsoever to do with my life having very little meaning unless you're in it."

He smiled and ran his fingers over the wedding ring on hers. "I love you, Doc." He didn't say it often. But he made sure she knew it every minute of every day.

"I love you." She kissed him quickly. "Now come on." She pulled him toward the picnic table, where the wedding cake was laid out on a pretty white cloth. "I'm not refereeing any battles between my father and Vivian, but they're all standing very close to our wedding cake. That's a recipe for disaster."

He chuckled and slid his hand over her back laid bare by the halter dress. "Sure you don't want to just get the heck out of here while the going's good?"

She slid him a look. "Don't tempt me."

"Are you?" He drew his fingertip along her spine.

She exhaled carefully, feeling heat race through her. "Very."

His lips tilted wickedly. "Good." He pulled her the rest of the way toward the cake just as Vivian handed the violin back to Casey.

"I never expected to hear this violin played again," she was telling him. "Not so beautifully."

"The only reason it's playable at all is because you got it fixed for me," Casey reminded her. "It means a lot to me and my family. It belonged to my grandmother, Sarah. She died a long time before I came along."

Hayley pressed her head against Seth's chest behind her and shared a smile with Jane. They both remembered when Jane had brought the broken violin to Vivian for help, even though she'd thought all was lost with Casey.

"I know," Vivian said in a shaking voice. She

sent Hayley a look that seemed filled with apology. "I know the violin belonged to your grandmother. Because it was my first husband who gave it to her." She turned the violin over and gently stroked the markings on the back. "And my father who gave it to him."

Casey's eyebrows pulled together and he let out half a laugh. "Talk about a small world."

"Not that small." Vivian swallowed and seemed to brace herself. "You see, my husband Sawyer Templeton was your grandmother's half-brother, dear. He just didn't know she existed until shortly after he and I married."

Hayley sucked in a breath.

Casey's stunned gaze flicked from Vivian's face to Hayley's. "Well, damn," he finally said, sounding just as dazed as she felt.

Seth's arms tightened around Hayley's waist. "Sounds to me like your family tree just got a whole lot bigger."

"And if I hadn't…interfered because she was

illegitimate and I was afraid of scandal," Vivian added, "half of everything that came from Templeton Steel would have been hers. Which is something I intend to finally rectify." She breathed deeply and raised her chin, looking skyward. "That's right," she said. "I'm going to get things right."

"Who's she talking to?" Hayley's brother had come up next to them.

"Dear Arthur," Hayley and Seth said together.

Arch shook his head. "She's a nut job."

"She's Vivian Archer Templeton," Hayley murmured. "That's your namesake, brother dear."

"Still a nut job." He headed toward Casey, his arm outstretched in greeting. "So. It sounds like we're cousins..."

* * * * *